Elen and the Water Goblin

Elen and the Water Goblin

Daniela Burley

D&D Burley

CONTENTS

CONTENTS

For my son Joe
For my daughter Isabelle
And for Erika and Silvia who were amongst the first to know

Acknowledgments

So much gratitude and love to my husband David and children for their continued support of my writing.

A big thank you to my mother-in-law Helen who has been ever so helpful and even at her busiest times she would support me.

Thank you, Mum for opening my eyes and seeing things can be different, for passing your creative genes onto me.

Thank you, Dad for being patient when I struggled to see the end of the tunnel.

Thank you to my sister Adriana for her encouragement and putting up with my nagging around writing.

Prologue

A myth told from generation unto generation about a Water Goblin, a green man that lived in ponds of the **Austro-Hungarian** monarchy, has just been rebuilt into a story. The story was inspired by author K. J. Erben, whose poem "Vodnik" – "Water man" – has touched many generations since the 18th century. In his memory, a new tale has begun…

A figure walked down a bumpy road that led to a village. A red ribbon hung freely from the dark green hat covering his face. He entered the village through a massive wooden gate. Two stone poles framed the gate securely.

The figure lifted his head to greet two guards standing not far from the gate and stammered, "Go-o-od d-day."

The guards simply stared at the newcomer whose face was of an unusual green colour.

The figure passed them and continued into the main square. His feet, frog limbs, made walking rather difficult. He staggered along the main road into the core part of the village. Many people were bustling around the main square where a market was held, chatting, buying groceries and exchanging products. The figure stopped in front of the market. With his right hand, also a frog limb, he took off his hat to reveal wispy, shoulder-length green hair.

"Good day," the green figure said loudly and more confidently, attracting attention.

The main square suddenly fell silent.

"A monster!" a child screamed, pointing at the strange figure with frog limbs and that unusual green face. The child grabbed his mother's hand, pulling it violently. He started shaking and crying uncontrollably.

"A monster!" another person echoed, followed by a chorus of, "It's a monster!"

The figure, who was around six feet tall and quite skinny, kept his posture straight. His eyes widened in surprise. He had never seen so many people before. Now they were frightening him, shouting something at him. He turned around to see the two guards rushing towards him.

What's happening? he thought to himself.

A man dropped his bags and picked up a stone. He threw it at the green figure, and it landed at his frog feet. Many more stones followed. The figure faced the two guards, bewildered and suddenly frightened. Stones hit his legs, and he felt an agonising pain. He placed one foot in front of the other, his body leaned forward and in a faster motion he began to move towards the main gate. One of the guards began to close in on him as he raced as fast as he could to escape. As he left, he could still hear the loud grumbling of the villagers.

Running clumsily, he didn't stop until he reached a pond deep in a nearby forest. Heart racing, breathing heavily, he tutted to himself. He paused before diving into the pond, and then leapt in, splashing water around the banks.

"What happened to the Water Goblin?" a couple of frogs sitting by the pond croaked to each other.

1

The Village

Hundreds of years had passed. In a village, an old cottage built from mud and straw stood near to a wild forest. I wiped the sweat from my forehead as I swept the wooden path in front of our house. My lengthy brown hair slipped around my neck, so I stood tall and forced it on to my back. I breathed in the warm dusty summer air which tickled my nostrils, and my eyes wondered at the surrounding houses and people working nearby.

My father sat in his chair. His slim body structure held very little flesh. Eight years ago, he had danced, smiled, played and joked about with me; these days he was very still.

At the end of the day I pointed above the forest at the sun sitting on a cushion of orange glow, preparing for sleep. "Papa, look. Isn't it beautiful?"

The old man's face was a blank stare, as if someone were painting his portrait, his eyes fixed on a spot in the far distance. His shrivelled lips remained sealed. Papa had not talked for years, not since Ma died, to be precise. Not because he refused to, but because he was unable to. He was not present most of the time.

My mother had searched high and low in the forests for special flowers and leaves that could cure my father's illness. A very strange-looking green and blue flower seemed to be one of those that made my fragile papa happier and healthier. I was eight when my mother died, and in the nine years that have passed those flowers have never been found again. About a year after Ma died, he became worse and now he could not walk without support.

I crouched next to my father's chair. "The sky looks beautiful from here," I said, smiling. I closed my eyes. Father, I wish you could speak at least. You are the only person I have left from my closest family. I have no siblings like all the other children in our village. My head still close to his, I whispered, "Let's take you in."

*

That night rain washed over the village. Water Goblin sat at the edge of the pond under an old willow, his frog feet immersed in the water. He laughed loudly, moving his legs up and down and spreading his arms to catch some raindrops, celebrating rain. When the sun set he dived into the pond.

*

The next morning, I went to the butcher's and grocery shop. At the corner of the main square I came across the boy I usually met on my errands. He was homeless and often begged for food. I placed some bread into his hands, like I had done many times before.

"Here you are," I said kindly. As I stepped away from the corner a large hand grabbed me by the shoulder.

"My dear," came a voice from behind me. "It is forbidden to feed these imbeciles. They carry disease which may then be passed on to you and others. No wonder your father is unwell—"

At the mention of my father, I spun round and came face to face with a large guard of very muscular stature. I swallowed my fear and said, "It is not for you to say who has given any illness to my father. Because it is not you who has judgement over health or sickness, but God." I turned and started to walk away. The boy had gone.

The guard looked around and not seeing the boy, he laughed at me as he mocked, "Will God help your father, girl? And that boy belongs in the children's home!"

I did not reply but felt the urge to cry for help. I have to be strong, I commanded myself. There is a cure to heal my father, such a cure to bring him back from wandering down the halls of his mind. I felt heat spreading down my cheeks leaving burning lines of salty liquid as I ran through country lanes to the lonely, secluded cottage near the dark forest.

"My dear, my dear, I am dying of fear that I shall not see you again," my father cried as I walked in, my cheeks flushed and still wet.

I dropped my basket full of shopping and hugged my father tightly, wiping my tears on his top. He had a tendency to utter strange words and phrases that made no sense at all. This time though, I kept his words in my heart. They were far too painful to be disregarded. I looked at the far corner of the room only to see the little boy from the town square curled up in a ball. His light brown trousers were torn at the knees and his white shirt hung loose, the sides and front also torn. His dusty blonde hair had not been washed for weeks if not months. I slowly walked towards him.

He suddenly rose to his full height and said, "I would like to stay, please."

I felt the boy's pain of not having anyone to look after him. "You may stay here with us as long as you desire," I heard myself say.

He hugged me tightly and whispered, "Thank you. You are very kind."

Over the next couple of weeks I got to know my new friend and named him Dash because he was inclined to dash off unexpectedly.

"They died two years ago," Dash said, in answer to my question one evening, as he stared at the table we sat at.

"I am so sorry to hear that. Did they have a name for you?" I asked gently.

"Oh, yes. Little Angel, Mum called me. Little Devil, Dad used to shout. I think Dash is just perfect." He smiled at me.

"Little Monster." I laughed, stroking his blonde hair.

*

Some days later Dash was helping my father into his favourite chair when there was a knock at the front door. I opened it and a guard strode boldly into the house, the same guard I had met some time ago at the town square. I would recognise his face anywhere.

He announced, "It is prohibited to keep street children. You also have no parents, as your father is unable to fend for or defend himself, let alone fend for you. If you are able to prove that he is capable of caring for you, you may stay, otherwise you and the street child will be taken to the children's home and your father to the madhouse. You have a fortnight. The ministry of Galonia."

Dash was hiding behind my father, although the guard had no power to remove him from our house. The guard turned and left, his shoulders straight, his armour immaculate. He held a sparrow in one hand and a rolled-up note in the other.

"I am the cause of this visit," cried Dash.

"No, my little friend. You have not caused them to arrive at my doorstep. They would have come anyway." I hugged Dash and kissed his forehead. "I need to set off on a journey before sunrise to look for a flower that will cure my father of this illness," I exclaimed, adding, "I need you to look after him while I am away."

Dash nodded, although his face turned white and his eyes opened wider. What if we get another visit from the ministry of Galonia? he thought.

I packed myself a tiny knot of food, bread and water; something to keep me going as I searched for the cure. I did not know how long it would take me, but I had to do something before the guard returned in a fortnight.

*

That night, I could not sleep. Did I still have a chance to save my father and Dash from being taken away by the ministry guards? I could not let my father be taken away. He would die in the madhouse. He is not mad! Tears ran down my cheeks.

2

The Forest Journey and Water Palace

Water Goblin stood still in his water palace bedroom. Facing a soil wall, he clicked his fingers. A drawer as long as ten feet opened, stopping inches in front of him. Green trousers hung freely in the air.

"M-agic," he stuttered.

His red, sticky, coarse and exceptionally long tongue unfolded. It made his speech unclear. It was one of the features he had inherited from the frog family. He began to open other drawers which contained his shirts, hats, vests and coats. All his outfits were various shades of green. Water Goblin chose his shirt, trousers and all other clothing and scanned himself from his feet to his stomach.

"Everyth-ing i-is w-w-well," he stammered.

With a click of his fingers, the drawers became a soil wall again. He placed a dark green hat with a red ribbon on his head. His thin greenish hair hung to just above his shoulders. He caressed it with his frog limbs and felt its texture through the balls of his fingers.

*

The next morning, I set off with a small knot of food tied in a blanket across my chest. The length of my bluish dress fell below my knees, and my full sandals made of animal skin covered my ankles. As I entered the dark forest that stretched over acres and acres of land, untouched by man, the only noise was the sound of branches cracking beneath my feet. It did not seem strange to me that birds did not sing here because the forest looked uninviting to any animal, except evil creatures. I held no fear in my heart except the apprehension for my beloved father and my newly found friend.

"Oh dear, dear," I gasped.

I had walked for hours and hours, and the deeper into the forest I ventured the darker it became as branches spread in all directions and barely allowed any sunlight to enter. My leg muscles hurt, my back ached, my breathing was heavy. I rubbed my eyes. Several tree trunks were of a thick, mighty structure, with a broad crust around them, probably thousands and thousands of years old. There were paper birches amongst the ash trees and elder trees, beech trees, elm trees and a mixture of other types of leafy trees. Hardly anything ever happened in the forest, but the stillness and the darkness made it frightening.

I followed strange trails made by animals, perhaps wolves or even bears. Other animals would be frightened to live around here, I thought. The trails led me further and further into the forest. I pushed a branch away from my face and paced the dark path. The sun began to set. Trees and wild berry branches surrounded me, their twigs prickling my skin as I moved through them. Stepping on tall grass, I found myself deep in the forest, although there was still no sign of the flower I was looking for.

So many of the trees look the same, identical even; there is no way I will remember my way back, I suddenly realised. I sat down under a mighty tree, away from the tall grass, and opened my knot with the small amount of food I had packed earlier. To my pleasant surprise I noticed some insects, ladybirds and other bugs heading towards me. They must have been attracted by the breadcrumbs falling on the soil. I observed them for a while, noticing how cautious the insects were. I dropped another crumb on purpose to see their reaction and then continued to eat. Once I had finished, a wave of tiredness overcame me. I rested against a tree and closed my eyes.

I was awoken by a howling sound many hours later. The forest was almost pitch black, but the lack of light did not frighten me and would not discourage me from continuing my search. The skies were clear, and the moon was out in its almost full glory, accompanied by stars whose slight glow helped guide my way. I continued my walk until I came to a steep hill. I looked around for a stick strong enough to support my weight. Breathing in the fresh air, I set off on a challenge.

I climbed the hill slowly, carefully taking one step at a time. Stones rolled away underfoot as I stepped on them. They fell to the bottom of the slope, creating echoes.

"Is there no end to this hill?" I uttered to myself, stepping on a larger stone as I gingerly carried on. I quickly glanced behind me and saw the bottom of the slope was extremely far away now. My head spun and I grabbed the rocks jutting out of the slope.

When I finally reached the very top, I sat down to rest. Squatted down in a ball, I hugged my knees and thought of Papa. He must be in one of his deep sleeps right now, unaware that his only daughter had nowhere to lay her head on this cool summer night. Papa would never have allowed me to go to the forest; I was forbidden to play near it when I was younger. Now I was here, I had to find the cure. I wanted to make him proud. No one will separate us, ever.

I stood up, determined to continue my search and find what I was looking for. The moon lit the road ahead. Despite the darkness I felt quite safe in the forest. It was as if someone were looking out for me.

*

Water Goblin observed the almost full moon as he squatted like a frog next to his pond amongst the tall grass, not visible to the human eye. From fireflies and frogs, he had heard that a beautiful young girl was heading his way, supposedly lost or looking for something.

The Water Goblin laughed to himself. She will be my companion, forever, he mused. He planned how to drown her, take her heart and place it in a jar. She will be mine soon. If I take her heart, she will not be able to feel the loss of her family, or love anybody she ever meets, he reflected.

He stood up to his full height and clapped his strange frog hands. They were green, just like the rest of his skin. The sound carried far beyond the pond and into the surrounding forests. With his new plan firmly in his mind he jumped into the green mould and disappeared beneath some lily pads. He swam just like a frog, spreading his arms and legs in all directions, until he reached the bottom of the pond. He then stood up without being swept or swayed by the pressure of the water. His large green frog feet and the membranes between his toes helped to keep him stable in the water.

At the bottom of the pond he pulled away a substantial boulder that acted as a door. Water Goblin stepped into the first room: a fair-sized waiting room that had never been used by humans before. Only frogs or fish were invited to his palace. It had soil walls with some exceptionally large rocks sticking out, which the Water Goblin used as shelving for plants. All kinds of plants were held in jars, pots and other strange-looking cans. In a far corner stood a stone that was used as a table, surrounded by smaller stones. The floor, made of soil and sand, felt as soft as carpet when Water Goblin walked on it. The room had no windows, but he caught some fireflies, placed them in jars and spread them all around the room. He remembered it was time to release them.

"Let's take you outside," he mumbled, observing a firefly sitting in a jar with her arms crossed. Each night he caught new fireflies for the next day. It was one of his daily chores.

He walked into the next room that was larger than the previous one. Water Goblin stopped at an outsized stone in the middle of the room and sat on one of the ten smaller stones around it. Water flowers and weeds growing on the walls caught his eye. He got up, and carrying some of the jars he had collected, he made his way into the last room.

This was as big as the previous room and had a tiny number of flowers growing on the walls. Weeds in the shape of a square on the floor was used as a bed. Water Goblin had no need for a pillow or covers as the water was usually warm, though this winter he felt the chill. The girl will make me a suitable cover for the winter chills, he said to himself, laughing loudly at the thought.

Tadpoles gathered around the front door, noisily poking their heads around the boulder.

"Le-eave me alo-one!" he shouted.

There was no kitchen in the palace. Water Goblin mainly ate flies, mosquitoes, moths and even dragon flies. After all, his tongue was formed to catch insects.

Water Goblin was able to talk for as long as he remembered. He was a good singer too, at least that is what he thought. He performed to a tiny audience of frogs, fireflies and fish. His singing comprised croaking sounds and laughing. He was proud of being able to entertain his small audience once a month, usually when the moon was in its full glory. He knew his laughter could be heard far beyond the forest, right into the village below. He enjoyed the thought of people being frightened by him; they were meant to fear him and never cross his pond. They were strange-looking creatures, killing animals in some parts of the forest he would never go to. Then they cooked them on a fire and ate them. His face drained of blood, his mouth opened and his tongue fell out at the thought. He mumbled, "Bad cre-a-atures!"

Many, many years ago he had tried to enter the village below the forest but was stoned away by its inhabitants, never to return. Hundreds of years had passed since then, but Water Goblin decided never to enter that village again. He would wait for them to come to his place, and he would treat them the way they had treated him. The girl coming his way, into his trap, would be his first revenge, a sweet revenge. She would be his companion, someone to share the chilly rooms with during the winter, someone to talk to through the lonely nights, someone to sing to...

"Ha, Ha, Ha!" He laughed above the pond, letting the fireflies out of the jars he had brought with him. "You are free..." He grinned sheepishly. He stumbled on some rocks but regained his balance instantly.

"She isn't f-a-ar from h-e-ere
She is o-on her way
She is on top o-of the h-i-il
She is not f-a-ar away."

Water Goblin sang a funny tune, dancing around the pond in slow wobbly movements, clapping his strange frog hands. He faced the pond as he entertained himself. He could feel tingles in his strange frog feet, in the balls of his toes. One foot up, one foot down, he skipped round and round the pond.

"This i-is your s-s-special song t-o-onight," he stammered.

His tongue got in the way as he tried to speak and it unfolded, making his pronunciation unclear. He sucked it back into his mouth, releasing some germs and white mucus from his mouth. How unpleasant, he thought to himself. Practising good manners, he pulled a handkerchief, green of course, out of his pocket and wiped his mouth clean. It would be shameful to be seen in such a state by a lovely young girl. His chanting was a bit quieter than usual because he did not want to let other creatures know what he was up to.

3

The Pond

Just before sunrise I lay against a tree trunk and dozed off.

I woke up as the sun was rising, surrounded by many insects: ladybirds, at least ten I counted, beetles, woodlice and other bugs, and some ants that wandered across my knot which still contained some bread. They seemed to have formed a protective circle around me.

Well, I thought, they must have been curious about my presence in this uninviting dark forest, which has never been approached by humans before. I caught sight of some squirrels playing, running from one tree to another. In daylight, the forest started to look more pleasant and real, as rays of sunlight slipped in through the tree trunks. Perhaps it was the darkness of night that made it seem more daunting and frightening.

The sun created rays of light through the trees, prodding me to continue my search. I picked up my blanket that had kept me warm in the night and carried my food during the day, and I set off.

It was not long before I exited the dark forest and saw before me a large plain which stretched for many acres. Far beyond that grassy plain was forest again. After numerous weary hours in the forest, it felt refreshing and warm to be in the sun. I saw so many different types of flowers such as cornflowers, clovers, lupines, popcorn-flowers, fiddle-neck flowers and other wild flowers, and I felt my heartbeat increase with excitement. Maybe this is it, maybe this is where my mother found the cure.

I could vividly remember the flower; it was different to any normal flower that grew in gardens and in fields. Its petals were of a rare shape, similar to a diamond, and there were five of them. One petal was green, and the others were half green and half blue, the colours more or less blending into each other. Most spectacular was the stem; it was bright yellow, like its leaves. You couldn't miss it.

I hopped excitedly from one leg to another in the grass and plants that reached to my waist as I enjoyed the full view of the sun. It seemed magical, yet I anticipated a different magic. My excitement was catching; some flowers were swaying with my skipping. I had almost reached the middle of the plain when I noticed a pond.

Would that water be clean enough to drink? I wondered. Even if it was not, I had no option but to find out for myself. The pond was surrounded by reed mace (bulrush) tall grass that was taller than me. It swallowed my tiny being, then released me two inches from the water.

"How strange," I said to myself. I turned around. I could have sworn this grass had hands that could easily push me into the pond. I sat down on the bank of the pond, took off my sandals and immersed my tiny feet into the green algae water. "This water will certainly cool my feet down," I muttered.

Suddenly a strange green hand, or something that looked like a hand, appeared on my right leg. It grabbed hold of me, pulling me into the pond. I fought back but its strength was no match for me.

Just before I was completely submerged, I screamed, "Sto-op!"

*

Water Goblin opened his eyes underwater and watched his prey fall, unconscious, to the bottom of the pond and her heart become his, exactly as he had planned. Admiring the heart, he carefully placed it in a glass jar. The heart was beating and looked healthy.

"Now it is mine to keep!" he smirked.

Water Goblin carefully lifted up the body and swam down to his castle, where he placed the girl gently on his weedy bed, stroked her hair and touched her nose. He cast a spell that erased her entire memory and suppressed all her feelings. In return, he gave her the ability to live underwater and made her his companion, his heartless companion. Then he waited in the next room.

*

Opening my eyes, I looked around me. My eyes widened at the sight.

"Am I underwater and still alive? Am I dreaming?" I touched the weed that I was sitting on and it tickled my fingers. I was alive, but somewhere strange, in a chamber decorated with flowers. "Who owns this place? Why am I here now?" I asked aloud.

Standing up, I swayed from left to right, trying to get used to walking under water. Swimming would be easier, I thought.

I smiled as though without a care in the world. I spotted an entrance to another room and headed towards it.

Although this place was unusual and not quite to my liking I could not put my finger on why I did not actually resent it. Being underwater, able to breathe and walk was more than incredible already.

I walked into a large room and saw some sort of seats on my left. On one of them sat a strange-looking figure. His head was bent over, his hat hanging off his head and covering his face. He seemed to be asleep, but my presence caused him to lift his head and stare directly into my blue eyes. His big green eyes pierced me, and instinctively I took a step back. With my hand over my mouth, I could not take my eyes off this stranger. He stood up and gestured for me to sit next to him.

Being a guest here, as I thought I was, I sat gently on one of the hard rocks that were specially designed for seating.

"Wel-lcome," Water Goblin began. "My name is Green Water Goblin. I have lived here ever since I can remember. This is my palace. Now you are to share it with me. You may enter any room you like, you may swim to the surface of the pond at night, but you are forbidden to rise to the surface in daylight."

His tongue got stuck at times and he stumbled over some words, but he never took his eyes off me. His voice was harsh. It carried through the waves right to my gentle ears.

I certainly would never forget his words or his staring eyes. Am I a prisoner of this creature? Trapped underwater in strange rooms with insufficient lighting, with no means of escape and no food to eat? How am I to survive around here?

Water Goblin stood up abruptly, put his hat back on his head and walked out of the room. Clearly, he was demonstrating that he owned the palace as well as the pond and no one was to argue with him, let alone a weak little girl.

"It is dark in this room lit only by fireflies, so how can I know when night falls? Am I to wait for his approval or arrival to be let out on to the earth's surface?" I mumbled to myself. Still sitting at the rock table, I dropped my head into my hands in despair. Looking up, I stared into the distance as if there were no walls in front of me. I had a vision of a poor old man and a child, but I did not recognise them.

What had happened to me?

*

Water Goblin was sitting on the bank of the pond, grinning from ear to ear, overjoyed with his achievement. His feet were immersed in the water and he gently moved them back and forth as if he were walking, creating waves and attracting small fish to play with him.

He thought about the forthcoming full moon's celebration that evening, where he would sing his songs and to which the girl would be invited. If she can dance with me as well, not only observe, then I might let her out to wander around the forests tonight, he considered. Goblin planned to get her to like him despite having stripped her of human feelings. He wanted her to listen to him and be around him at all times.

Night fell, and the moon and stars appeared in the clear skies. It was time for the girl to surface. Water Goblin summoned his team of fish.

"Bring the girl to me," he ordered.

*

The fish gently swam with me to the surface of the pond and then left me to reach for Water Goblin's hand. Reluctantly, with closed eyes and lowered head, I reached out to him. The gentle tips of my fingers touched his muscular palm; he locked the balls of his fingers into my palm and pulled me out.

It was a magical moment for Water Goblin, something he had longed for over the years.

With no feelings of resentment, I joined Water Goblin at his side.

Frogs gathered on lily pads, sitting impatiently, staring at the pair. Fireflies flew above the pond, creating a spectacular circle of lighting for the show. Fish somersaulted for the parade; insects and other small animals gathered around the pond, there were rabbits and squirrels as well as bats and owls sitting on the further trees. They were not invited to join the celebration which only involved singing and dancing but were curious as to what was happening at the pond. The croaking started and Water Goblin sang his first song:

"We cele-ebrate together
With flies and fireflies
And others from the fore-est
The arrival of a dearest
Girl from hu-uman world!"

His chanting echoed into the forest and surrounding mountains, from which the howling of hungry wolves could be heard in return. The howling persisted for a while, and at times seemed louder than the goblins' chanting. This irritated Water Goblin, although he never showed it, even in the slightest.

"May I?" Water Goblin asked, and with all his strength he swept me off my feet in a dance manner. We spun around the banks of the pond for many hours. I tried carefully not to tread on Water Goblin's feet that were exposed, naked.

Several hours later, the show stopped, all the animals dispersed into their places of living and only I was left standing, feeling rather lonely, next to the pond.

"You may go for a walk, but you must return to the pond before the sun rises. Do not wander off beyond the forest's hills that are far from my vision," Water Goblin warned.

4

Forest Queen

I had the whole night ahead of me to wander through the lonely-looking grounds of the forest. My only companions were fireflies, which were most probably the spies of my new master, Green. They followed me everywhere I went. Are they here to guard me or spy on me? Wolves howled in the distance, but animals did not frighten me.

I had been walking through the trees for some time when I heard a gentle voice say, "This way." I turned around to see who the voice belonged to, but I could not see anyone. "No, no, this way," the voice said again.

So I turned sharply to the left and followed instructions from the unknown source, and so did the fireflies. Was it them? I wondered. I passed many birch trees of the same build and height. At times I touched their branches, other times it seemed as though they wanted to touch me, reaching for my arm or cheek. It was odd to think they could be alive. It even looked like some birch trees were communicating with each other. I rubbed my eyes and watched the trees again to be sure, but this time everything was still, not even the leaves on the trees fluttered.

"How strange," I uttered. "I must be very tired." To my surprise, as I turned back to continue my walk, I noticed a rather oversized ancient oak tree with a mighty trunk, thick branches and large leaves. It looked different to any other tree, and it swayed gently from side to side, as if it were dancing with the wind. My jaw dropped and my eyes widened when I realised the tree was breathing. As I came closer the shape of a mouth formed on the trunk.

"A tree with a mouth? How could that be?" I asked out loud.

It was not my imagination – the tree was real. It was breathing and had a mouth. Suddenly two large holes appeared, and a pair of eyes gawked at me. I did not fear things that appeared unusual, but I did wonder about the surroundings and the reality that I now found myself in.

As I approached the tree it spoke gently in a woman's voice: "Hello, dear."

I stopped in my tracks and gazed into those eyes. "How...?"

"It's all right, my dear. I really am talking to you. How is that possible, you ask? You are under a spell that enables you to see me in my different life form. You are also able to live underwater, I have heard."

"Oh, hello... Well, it's true that I can survive underwater. Who could you have heard that from?" I asked.

"Your beauty has been spoken of by many animals and insects all around me. I am only wise to listen."

"Although you are not a human your wisdom is to be admired. The truth you speak and the energy that glows around you make you so mysterious," I complimented the tree before adding, "Who are you?"

"I am the Queen of the forest. I reside in this part of the forest. This spot is the best position for me to see what is happening with my fellow tree ladies and tree gentlemen. I guard them from bad influences, weather and any form of magic."

"You are a wise tree. Would you know why I wandered away from humans into these dark forest grounds?" I probed.

The tree closed its eyes. "Something brought you over to this wild forest. You were seen searching for a flower. A flower that has powers no human has ever known. It is one of its kind and grows only once in a whole year. Should you wish to find it, you will need the help of a strong individual. The tree paused for a moment. "It seems that someone is in need of a special power to awaken them from a deep sleep."

"There is an old gentleman I can see in my vision. He seems sad and alone. Bless his soul," I exclaimed.

"The man may be your close relative, or someone you know very well otherwise you would not approach this dark forest alone," the Queen said harshly.

"I have no memory of him. I only have recollections at times," I said.

"Your memories have been blurred. It was Water Goblin. He used his spells on you. His spells are not powerful in our world, but they may do much harm to humans. Humans are especially susceptible. You don't need to be too afraid; his spells are only effective up to the banks of the pond. He would be unable to use them around here, but he can use others to help him pursue his target. Beware of his wrath. If you wish to come back this way, do not upset him," the Queen cautioned.

I nodded, listening patiently.

"There is a friend of mine that may be able to help you. Squirrel is very talkative but quick to deter bad creatures from harming anyone in his protection. He will accompany you to meet the fastest transport in or around the forest, and that is the reindeer. The greatest of the great, the fastest of the fast... Squirrel and the reindeer will be your guide on your search. This is the only way I can help you, my dear. But beware, there are bad creatures around the forest."

At that moment, the tree froze and the eyes and mouth disappeared. The Forest Queen had reverted to an ordinary large ancient oak tree, one to admire for many hours. I realised I had not even said thank you and muttered, "Thank you, my Queen..."

I became aware of the fact that I must have spent some time talking to the Queen of the forest and decided to start making my way back to the pond. Water Goblin would get angry if I was not back before sunrise. Fireflies even now danced above my head.

The birch trees still looked pretty similar to each other, but now not a single branch moved. Anyone could easily get lost in this forest! It's as if the paths had been deliberately covered up, I thought to myself.

When the girl had left the Forest Queen, the fireflies remained. The Queen opened her eyes again.

"Keep her safe," she commanded.

"We will, we will, Queen," the fireflies answered.

The Queen waved her branch hands at them as they left. She could hear them giggling happily, dancing around, without a care in the world.

*

My dress was dry now, as well as my hair. I hadn't even noticed my clothing was wet. Despite not knowing what might appear in my path during such a dark night, I walked without fear and with confidence, looking straight ahead. Branches cracked under my feet as I walked towards the pond. I tried to remember the shape of each tree I passed. In my head I was marking my way back. One day I might need to return to the Forest Queen.

Up ahead I noticed something tiny in my path: it was some kind of animal. It was staring back at me defiantly, its eyes unwavering and shining vividly. As I drew closer, I recognised its features.

"A squirrel," I gasped.

This very dark night there was a lonely squirrel in my path. How incredibly strange. Then I remembered the Forest Queen's instructions which included something about a squirrel, a talkative squirrel. Could this be the one she meant?

"Hello, my dear. Yes, I know you are puzzled by the fact that I am talking to you but you are surprised more by my unusual nightly appearance as we squirrels do not wander the forests in the night—" the squirrel began.

If I had not interrupted him by asking, "You are the Forest Queen's friend, aren't you?" he would have happily continued for hours explaining why squirrels do not run around in the night.

"My name is Red. I have been named after the extraordinary colour of my fur. As you can see, if you can see in this darkness, three quarters of my body is of a very bright red colour, only my tail has a light brown touch. Not that I am proud of my appearance, but don't you think I look adorable?" Red surprised himself asking for an approval. He then spun around and waggled his tail.

"Oh, yes, you do—" I agreed.

Very confidently Red cut me short and continued his speech. "Would you mind me hopping on to your shoulder as you are so very tall, and it would be rather awkward for you to constantly be bending down in order for you to hear me better? You can walk comfortably while I sit on your shoulder talking to you," Red said.

"Yes, of course you can," I answered.

Red hopped on to my back, gently pressing his nails into my dress, barely catching his step and nearly slipping as he climbed on to my left shoulder and then sat there with his upper paws crossed over his chest. He wiggled his bum a few times and once he was comfortable, he carried on talking.

"So you have had the pleasure of meeting the Forest Queen in her full glory? She does not appear in her natural self just to anyone. You must have had a spell put on you by someone. Actually, definitely, because I am talking to you and you can understand me." Red chuckled as he followed Queen's instructions.

I walked carefully and unhurriedly, smiling to myself, thinking how strange it must look with a squirrel sitting on my shoulder talking to me. I found his chatter rather entertaining.

Without waiting for my response, he continued to talk. "You must be a very brave girl to wander around this side of the forest. This part of the deep forest has not yet been approached by humans due to their fear of Green, the Water Goblin, and other unusual creatures. I can recall just a few sightings of a lady coming this way, and many, many years ago there was a gentleman wandering around here. Though I am unsure what happened to him. Some say he drowned in the pond, some say a spell was cast on him by Green, others say he saw the Forest Queen talking. There are many different rumours, but he did not return to this forest ever again."

He paused for a while just to see if I was interested in his tales, and when I looked up at him with my dark blue eyes he blushed and resumed his conversation.

"I am talking quite a lot and have not yet let you say a word. Would you tell me what brings you here?"

"I do not remember anything that happened before I woke up on a strange bed made of grass in water that was green, in something that resembled a room, in a pond in the middle of nowhere," I said, struggling to make sense of it as I said it out loud.

"Oh dear, dear. It's worse than I thought. What are the chances that you could remember anything when a spell of such magnificent strength was cast on you by Green? He wants to ensure that you never leave that pond; he wants you to understand that you can only belong underwater because you are able to live underwater. He is an old crafty Water Goblin you should be wary of. Don't be fooled by his appearance," Red warned. "I believe the Forest Queen gave you a clue about the reasons you might have entered this forest." Red paused. "We are nearly at the pond. I must leave you here. If Green spots me talking to you he will not let you out for many months. You, my dear, have a rest and think about the reason you had entered this forest. If your feelings are strong enough you may be able to break one of his spells.

The spell he cast on your memory, perhaps? I will see you again before long, my dear."

Red patted my cheek gently and hopped on to a nearby tree that separated the fields, where one lonely pond stood, and the other side was many miles of dark forest. Red was sitting on a branch at the level of my head. He gawked into my blue eyes once more, this time without blushing and added, "I shall see you tomorrow. Once you enter the forest I shall know. I shall find you, I am always nearby. Cheerio..."

Then he waved his tiny right paw at me and hopped off the tree, scurrying away into the forest. I watched him until he disappeared into the darkness.

"A talking squirrel. A talking tree. A Water Goblin in a pond," I said, bewildered.

"It must be a thrill.

It seems unreal.

Spells cast by Green.

He must be very mean."

I gasped in disbelief. I was puzzled, I could not remember much any more. The old man and a young boy from my vision were fading away. Who am I? Where do I belong? I remembered Red's words which clearly stated that Water Goblin wanted me to see it this way; he was playing tricks on my mind. I walked slowly, recalling every word and every event of tonight's adventure. Red had asked me to think hard about the reason I had entered the forest in the first place.

"Why do I need a flower? Who is this man I see in my vision?" I asked myself aloud.

Entering the pond carefully, right foot first, then left, I walked further away from the bank, into the middle of the pond. The water reached my chin, then I took another step forward and my whole body disappeared underwater. I could see and easily navigate around the pond with the help of the moon.

Fireflies above the pond produced extra light for me; they were probably not even aware they were doing so. They followed me everywhere I went, and I could get into trouble if they spoke to Water Goblin about my outing. Would they do such a thing? Whose friends were they?

5

Hunger

I dived to the bottom of the pond and stood up. I faced the large boulder that was the entrance to Water Goblin's palace, a pond palace! Everything stood still in the pond, all the fish were asleep. I picked up a tiny rock from the bottom of the pond and used it to knock on the strange door. One, two, three... again, knock, knock, knock. After a while the large rock started to move towards me. The noise had woken the fish as plenty were now gathered around me, patiently waiting with me to enter the palace.

Goblin appeared at the doorway and said, "We-elcome ba-ack," as he waved me in.

Goblin's affection for me did not extend towards the nosy fish. He frowned at them furiously as I entered, careful not to let me notice. The fish stopped before Goblin, angrily opening their mouths, breathing indignantly at his lack of hospitality. He waved his right hand at them, hushing them away from the doorway.

"Can't I get so-ome privacy so-ometimes? Do you ha-ave to disturb me-e e-every minute?" Goblin gave an angry sigh. He did not think for a moment the fish would be as curious as he was about me.

I passed the front room without stopping and entered the sleeping room. I stopped at the grassy bed. Dropping down, I let the weight of my body bend my knees. I lay sideways, lifeless on the weedy bed, then curled up in a ball.

*

Water Goblin pulled in the boulder and walked into the room where the girl was already fast asleep. My guest can have that room, he thought. He did not feel sleepy as he preferred to lie on the banks of the pond, in the soft grass that stretched on one side. He loved to gaze at the moon each night. Chasing fireflies and swimming in the pond were his favourite hobbies during the day. Water Goblin decided that he would go over the surface and risk falling asleep until the sun woke him up. Anyway, there were no other strange creatures to discover him asleep during the day which he could possibly frighten, and humans did not ever walk these grounds unless they were as brave as his guest. He laughed as he lay on the grass next to the pond.

"S-stunning," he mumbled. "Extraordinary circumstances," he added, remembering how he had gained a companion for himself. Looking at the motionless moon, its shape, his eyes narrowed, a smile formed on his face and his shoulders dropped towards the ground as he exhaled. He imagined being in the universe walking on the stars. He enjoyed the idea and toyed with the notion until his eyes closed and he dreamed about his freedom in the universe.

*

When I woke up my stomach rumbled.

"Ah, I need to eat," I said to myself. The grassy bed was soft, very comfortable to sleep on, but I needed energy which I lacked due to not eating for many, many hours. The only food I knew of was human food.

"Somewhere there is a blanket with bread wrapped in it." I could just recollect carrying it. Before I had immersed my feet in the water I had placed it by the pond, in the tall grass. "Oh, I must look for it, I have to eat something."

I intended to go over the surface of the pond as soon as possible even if the sun had already risen. I walked into the front room where I saw fireflies in the jars glowing dimly, projecting a very small amount of light for me to see. The room seemed empty. Water Goblin was nowhere to be seen, so I continued into the corridor room which separated the front room and the boulder at the entrance. The boulder was huge, and I mentally prepared myself as I knew it would take all my strength to open. My determined mind would not give up on food that my body desperately needed. I walked over to the stone very confidently and pushed it as hard as I could. To my amazement it gave way and let me out into the pond.

I fully expected the nosy fish to gather around me as they would have felt the vibrations of my movement. And as if they could read my thoughts, they swam around me in an instant.

"Ah, you little cheeky monsters," I exclaimed. "I need to get my food from the bank of the pond without the Goblin's knowledge. I don't expect your help but please don't tell him that I went up otherwise he will be angry with me," I begged.

They must have understood because they started to pull away from me, swimming in different directions, letting me swim freely without attracting the attention of any other creatures. Water Goblin's presence was unknown at that moment. He could only be above the pond, I imagined. I swam gently to the surface, and then popped my head out just enough to search for Water Goblin.

"He is not around the pond," I mumbled to myself. Even if Water Goblin was somewhere around the pond I would not be able to spot him amongst the tall grass. I swam until I reached the bank on one side of the pond where I quietly pulled myself out of the water and squatted, hiding in the tall reed mace grass.

"Now, it's time to look for the blanket," I said quietly as I squatted my way around the pond. "It has to be here some-where." The grass was more or less the same shape and length all around the pond. "I have no time, I must hurry." I searched and searched until I caught a glimpse of a white garment. "That must be it," I exclaimed, smiling excitedly. I opened the knot. The bread was still fairly fresh as I examined it. At that moment I felt something move right next to me.

*

Water Goblin could sense the vibration of movement in the grass, which woke him up. He stood tall, directly opposite the girl, staring furiously into her pale face. This human creature has only spent one day underwater with me and already she has dis-obeyed my orders, he thought. Before he could say a word, the girl started to explain.

"Mr Green, I had no food to eat for a while, and this little ration I had left above the pond's palace was the only means of keeping my strength up. There is no need for you to punish me as

you know I had no intention of disregarding your strict orders."
She smiled for the first time.

She is either smarter than me, or she is just an honest person,
Water Goblin thought.

He could not know just yet, but the girl's smile worked mir-
acles on Goblin's attitude. His face softened and he managed to
twist his mouth into some sort of grin, making it clear that she
would not be punished for her bravery this time.

"The r-reason for you b-being hungry h-has been ac-cepted.
This was only t-the f-first and must be the l-last time you will
disob-bey me. A-any further b-breaking of my rules and you will
be p-punished." As usual, when he spoke his tongue unfolded
many times, causing him to stumble over his words.

The girl certainly did not find it funny but rather intimidat-
ing as his green eyes never left hers, not even for a split second.
He let her eat the bread while he dragged her by her left hand
towards the pond. He lifted each foot in turn, slowly like they
might have had weights tied to them. This gave the girl time to
enjoy the little food she had, not knowing when she would eat
again.

"We shall feast tonight," Goblin yelled.

It appeared she would have something to eat after all.

Goblin let go of the girl's arm as they arrived at the edge of the
pond. He clapped his frog hands, and countless fish and frogs as-
sembled around him. He mumbled unclear orders to them and
off they all went; the fish disappeared into the pond and the frogs
into the tall grass.

6

The Feast

Just before joining the feast preparation I waited for the sun to set. I sat on the grassy bed recalling my conversation with the Forest Queen and Red the squirrel. Red had asked me to think about why I had wandered into this side of the forest that was never visited by humans, except for a few lost souls. As hard as I tried, it was difficult to see or imagine anything before seeing Water Goblin's green face. What flower did the Forest Queen mean? Why a flower?

"Except, except, oh yes, I did remember where my blanket was. How did I do that?" I gasped. It had been a strong need for food that made me recall where my last portion of food was. "How can I invoke a similar need so that I can remember something about the purpose of my trip?"

I stood up suddenly with that thought in my mind and looked around the room that was nearly dark now. At that moment, Water Goblin walked in and allowed me to go above the pond.

"It's very da-ark in here," said the Goblin. "T-the fireflies are not pr-rodu-ucing any light. They will die if we do-on't let them out." He swallowed the saliva that had started to run down the corners of his mouth and placed some jars into my arms, before gesturing for me to follow him.

Above the pond the sun began its descent, creating an orange shadow around its shape. Fireflies, the Goblin's providers of light, flies, daddy-long-legs, and many other bugs gathered food on to some large boulders. Beyond the tall grass boulders and rocks acted as tables and chairs.

I admired all the tiny insects gathering nuts, berries of all kinds, even tiny wild strawberries that smelled awesome. I was now in the middle of the rush; I greeted the animals around me, saying, "Hello" and "Hello there." Pulling a secret smirk I remembered there was a way to beat that spell cast on my memory. I hopped from one foot to the other towards some large rocks, still carrying some jars in my hands.

I saw berries of all kinds being placed on large leaves, and some zucchini flower top that carried spring water was placed on the large boulders. It was yellow; a very bright yellow that struck me.

I came to a sudden halt as a flash of a flower with very bright yellow leaves and stem sprang into my mind. Dropping the jars, I stood still and stared at the yellow top. All the animals that had been rushing around now stopped what they were doing and looked at me curiously.

"Oh, no," I mumbled.

This kind of action will attract Water Goblin and he will have many questions that I will not be able to answer. I do not understand why I saw a flower in my vision just now.

"Oh, it's all right. I am ok," I said calmly, picking up the broken glass.

My foot was bleeding. The broken glass had slashed through my sandal and blood now seeped through. If the animals were distracted further from their work, it would definitely attract Water Goblin's attention, so I squatted to pick up the rest of the broken glass and with my dress carefully wiped the cut.

The fireflies flew out from the jars I had dropped. "Thank you... thank you..." they whispered quietly, before flying away.

I need to find new jars otherwise I won't be able to explain what happened. Where did Water Goblin find glass jars? The only place I could think of was the village, and villagers were afraid of these dark forests. Who could have brought them here then?

I sensed and recognised the presence of a large person behind me. Water Goblin was looking at the broken glass in my hands.

"Can I explain?" I stammered.

"It happens to me-e al-l the t-time," he said. "I have many spares in the palace. There is a cupboard that opens by pulling a rock. I keep them in there." The only cupboard that was visible to anyone else, he thought.

He held out his green hands towards me. His palms were large. Observing the strange balls at the end of each of his fingers I placed the glass in his palms without looking into his eyes.

"The foxes get them from the village after hunting. They always bring some to me," Goblin explained proudly.

He carried the glass carefully away from the pond into the nearby forest and dug a hole in the ground. He placed them in the ground and covered them with ample soil; animals might cut their feet if he left the glass lying about. I could not believe my luck.

Walking about the feast preparation area and not helping was not what I was comfortable with. It was difficult to know if the animals understood me or if they were scared of me. I thought I should help but something was stopping me. I tried not to ogle at the yellow-coloured zucchini flower top because it transported me to some unknown state. My brain had a power over my actions. It wanted me to go closer and see it better. I had no choice but to do what my brain wanted. The need was as powerful as the need I felt when hunger overtook me.

Cautiously, I got very close to the yellow flower top. I sat on a small rock that was meant for seating, leaned towards a boulder that acted as a table and placed my elbows on it. I locked my face in my palms and let my memory flow as I stared at that yellow zucchini flower top.

I saw a man that was unable to communicate with me, I saw a boy with blonde hair, I saw an old lady with very similar facial features to my own, I saw a house in a village that was as neat on the outside as it was on the inside, I saw a guard coming to the house—

"Nice flower, isn't it? We use it as a water jug." Goblin's voice intruded into my thoughts.

He placed his left hand on my right shoulder as if to let me know I was here with him, not there in the human world, and as for my knowledge I will never be able to go back.

"Very clever," I agreed. "Although if you have all these jars locked away in a cupboard, unused, you could consider using them as water jugs. Just a thought," I added, respectfully.

"The case is that the j-jars m-may be a h-hazard to the clumsy a-animals. Their paws are not as strong a-as human's ha-ands and they are not designed for ho-olding fragile a-articles in them," Goblin argued, now sitting opposite me at the table.

I lifted my head and looked directly into his green eyes. Strange, he is most probably able to see in the dark very well though he wishes to catch fireflies on a daily basis to light his home, I reflected.

A frog leapt on to the stone table and turned to face Water Goblin. The frog mumbled some words that I was unable to understand and sprang off again.

Goblin snorted and said, "Would you excuse me, please? I have something to take care of," and walked away.

The yellow flower top was removed by a team of frogs and replaced with a bright red flower top. The table was one of the first in a long row of tables. Names were written on leaves in golden paint and placed on seats. Each leaf had a walnut placed on it, probably for a reason. A frog placed a leaf on the table where I was sitting. It read: "The guest". I thanked the frog and smiled. It grinned back, displaying its long pinkish tongue. Nice greeting frog, I thought.

There were nuts of many kinds. I wondered what other animals would be invited to the feast. Frogs only ate flies, and they did not seem to be included on the menu, well, not just yet. As if reading my thoughts, another large leaf was placed before me. There were strange larvae and slimy worms of many colours wriggling about the leaf. My stomach turned over at the thought of consuming them, although I was not horrified. My knowledge was wide therefore I understood it was common for animals to consume larvae.

Frogs, some squirrels, rabbits, foxes, badgers and other animals took their named seats. Two foxes sat next to me, one on each side. They were very friendly with Goblin earlier and I noticed a crafty smirk on their faces. Maybe that was how they always looked, but I would not trust them outside of the feast.

Goblin walked around the many stone tables ensuring there was sufficient food and that it was spread evenly amongst the animals. Many animals smirked at him, bowed their heads and shook his green hand. He treated them with respect in return and they acknowledged his efforts praising him tenderly. Are these animals his friends, army, or what? I could not decide. I observed Water Goblin. He was now approaching my table, shaking many paws before he stopped at my seat. He bowed to me and offered me his right hand. I placed my right hand in his palm and watched him as he kissed the back of my hand. Every animal clapped in support of this gesture.

Goblin smiled warmly. He stood at the top of the rows of tables where everyone could see him and stammered:

"With delight and ple-easure
Eat to a gr-reat me-easure
Food pr-roduced by nature
Eat well, it's o-our c-culture
To our g-guest and to you my friends."

He held up a red flower top, in which water was mixed with some pollen. Taking a gulp of the liquid, he scanned the feast area noticing that everyone except me was drinking their liquid. I pressed the strange cup to my lips but did not dare taste that mixture. Goblin visibly gazed at me, giving me no choice but to taste it. I gobbled it quickly in order to avoid any strange taste, but was pleasantly surprised by its sweetness, rather like honey.

"Oh, that was unexpected," I remarked. After a few minutes my vision blurred slightly. I started to smile.

Goblin laughed loudly. He had made her drink the celebration drink with the spell of happiness in it.

I ate many berries and nuts and picked at some worms from the leaf I had intended not to even look at let alone eat from. The spell was powerful. It made me want to dance. Goblin started singing with some frogs croaking in a strange tune.

"The feas-st, full of gues-sts
Wa-ater in flowers, food on le-eaves
Se-eats made of stones-s
Tonight there will nothing be lef-ft
Until everyone is gone."

Goblin noticed me talking to the foxes sitting either side of me. He knew I could understand them but was afraid the foxes would mention the village, villagers or anything that could evoke any memories and therefore significantly affect his spells. He approached me with a grin on his face.

"Would you dance with me?" he requested.

"Certainly," I replied.

Goblin was not very good at dancing; I, on the other hand, enjoyed dance movements. His feet got in my way and I found myself stepping on his green ball toes most of the time. I apologised constantly. Frogs were croaking in some unknown tune though I got the gist of it immediately and tried to dance without making it more awkward for Water Goblin.

Many animals danced their dances which involved chasing each other's tails, jumping into the air and other strange moves. Then unexpectedly, the sound of howling wolves broke through, not far from the feast. Goblin stopped dancing and gazed into my blue eyes. I saw both anger and panic in them. The croaking stopped too.

Goblin let go of me and waved his arms up and down to hush the animals. Suddenly a large wolf jumped out of the nearby forests and raced towards Goblin and me. I watched the huge animal closing in, heading straight for me. I did not move a muscle, but Goblin pushed me aside. He stumbled and fell, then started off against the large wolf. The animal turned towards me this time, it was reaching me fast. As the animal leapt into the cold night air Goblin stood in its way to intercept its impact on me. Mr Green was hit extremely forcefully by the wolf's large paw and was sent flying backwards before hitting the ground hard, pulling me with him.

The wolf stood above my lifeless body. It licked my face and I opened my eyes. Lifting its head towards the sky he howled for a while. Then it lifted its paw and scratched my left cheek with its long nails. Blood began to flow down my neck, but the wolf only howled. It gnarled at me, staring into my eyes then leapt into the air again. The wolf disappeared swiftly into the distance, far into the forest.

Goblin was still unconscious when I approached him. I asked the frogs to pour water on his face. "Use the jugs, the flower jugs." I pointed at the flower tops they were using as jugs and cups. More than twenty frogs jumped about, panic-stricken, trying to revive their master.

*

A loud croaking discussion started to take place at the table. I heard the word "guest" one too many times, and I started to think it was me who had attracted the unwanted attention of a predator.

Goblin stood up, still a bit shaken from the attack though he did not show it for long. The discussion that was taking place so eagerly ended as soon as Goblin walked towards the table. Mr Green swept the table clean with his arm. All the berries, nuts, leaves and flower tops flew into the distance and on to the floor. The frogs sitting at the table stared blankly at Water Goblin, their eyes wide open and faces drained of colour. Goblin calmed down a bit realising his guest might be watching him and said in my direction, "You may go into the pond. Wash the blood off your cheek and neck. Then I shall explain whom we have just encountered."

I left and did as I was told.

To everyone else, Goblin stated, "We are to protect this human life. She is in our possession and we shall give up our lives in order to keep hers safe. Does everyone understand?"

The frogs croaked loudly in agreement. Then one of them asked, "If she was not in our possession would WOLF have approached our feast?"

Goblin answered, "You fool! Of course not, he is after her. He can use her either as a feast or as a slave for him and his nasty gang!" Goblin placed both hands on the table as he scrutinised the frog.

The frog shouted, "He did not take her with him when he had the chance to do so! You were knocked out. It only howled at her and cut her face!"

"By cutting her face he marked her out. The fresh wound will attract his accomplices. You are all to look out for any suspicious movements around the forest from now on. I want to be informed about any stranger that approaches our place," Goblin instructed.

He knew what he'd just said was not true. The wolf wanted the girl to be afraid and run away into the village. That was his intention, as humans were not welcome in the forest.

"She is entitled to go wherever she chooses this night and every night unless she disobeys one rule: she must return before sunrise. You had better ensure she does otherwise you will all be punished," Goblin shouted.

The frogs were frightened. Foxes were leaving the discussion table with their heads bowed. They knew Goblin was not fooling around; he meant every word he said as well as those unsaid. The animals could read between the lines: think carefully before you disobey Water Goblin. Your life has an expiry date as from today. Those were Water Goblin's unsaid words.

Goblin seemed greener than usual, and his cheeks flushed a darker green. He did not get red with anger, he got greener. His frog soldiers, his green army, were useless unless he used his spells to make them powerful. This was his intention for the next battle against this large predator.

Suddenly Goblin remembered his guest was hurt down in his water palace. He left the table, his coat swinging about his body with his sudden movements as he headed towards the pond, leaving the frogs to ponder their actions, or rather their insufficient actions.

7

The Gift

Goblin entered the palace, still angry. He saw the girl sitting on the bed in the last room, her head bent low. Goblin walked into the room, then squatted down and gently lifted up her head to see the scar better. He touched it with the tips of his right-hand fingers and the scar disappeared.

"Beware of the wolf family. They are wild in nature and uncaring when hungry. They are a disgrace to the forest. If you wish to explore outside tonight you may go now." He spoke tenderly.

I had an idea in my head which I kept secret from everyone. The idea needed to be realised. Nothing would stop me from going into the forest and talking to Red or the Forest Queen, and no evil wolf family would distract me from realising it.

Goblin stood up. He opened a secret cupboard on the left of the entrance to the room and pulled out a handkerchief. He handed it to me. It was green with flowers knitted into all corners of it. I held it for a moment, admired it then popped it into my pocket. The handkerchief must have some magical power that Goblin does not want to mention otherwise he would not have given it to me.

"Oh, thank you," I gasped finally.

Goblin could not work out if she was shocked by the assault, or if she had other plans which would mean she had broken his spell but was managing to keep very cool about it.

"Are you well?" he enquired.

"Yes, I am fine. It was a surprise to be involved in an attack. I can't work out what I feel or what I should feel or if I feel anything at all!" I replied.

Goblin tried to sound reassuring. "There is nothing to worry about, my dear. You go and enjoy yourself tonight. My gift shall protect you from any danger. Just carry it with you at all times."

I avoided Mr Green's eyes, my head bent low. I was bothered by what had happened earlier: the wolf had not killed me or even taken me with it. It had struck me with its claws, causing me harm, but had not killed me. Goblin had been struck unconscious by his attacker. What lesson should I learn from this? At any cost, the wolves were dangerous species; I should protect myself from them.

Fireflies were illuminating the rooms again. Goblin must have caught them before the celebration had started.

I walked towards the front door and said, "I shall see you before the sun rises, Master," looking directly into his eyes, letting him know I would be fine on my own in the forest.

The palace was rather claustrophobic for two people and I needed my space. I also wanted to find out more about the new outside world that I had caught a glimpse of last night.

As Goblin let me out, he muttered, "Bye..."

I did not catch his words but waved politely before swimming towards the surface of the pond.

*

Walking into the forest, I looked around in every direction calling out "Red" as quietly as I could. I walked further and further into the forest and then came to a stop. There was a single tree trunk, most probably destroyed by lightning. It had a straight surface on one side and a tall sharp bit on the other, which resembled a seat. I sank, exhausted, on to the tree trunk. Then I tried again.

"Red, Red... Red," a tiny voice above my head started calling. The fireflies were flying above my head again. Red had said he would know when I entered the forest.

"Hello, my dear. I heard your calling in my deep sleep. I didn't realise I had taken a nap. Deeply sorry for my lateness." Red had appeared from nowhere, and now confidently hopped on to my left shoulder, as if he'd known me forever.

"I nearly lost hope of ever finding you," I said, exaggerating a bit, and giggled, making Red go even redder in than he already was.

"You know I am only ever two steps away from you, don't you, little girl?" He giggled too, and off we went deeper into the forests. Red pointed out which direction to go in and which parts of the forest to avoid. He mentioned bears and he also warned that some species of the wolf family were not very friendly.

"Some? So other species are? How could wolves be friendly towards any other animals if other animals are their prey?" I questioned, utterly puzzled.

"Yes, we may be their prey," Red began, "but there are some wolves that do not see us in this way. They see us as friends and would not hurt us."

I laughed at this but trusted Red to be telling me the truth. "Or they could consider eating grass?" I suggested.

Red laughed and laughed, covering his mouth with his tiny paws. When we had both stopped laughing we found ourselves in front of an uninviting wall of holly trees with spiky leaves.

Up to now I had been enjoying myself but now the situation was starting to get a bit scary. How could we possibly continue any further without being scarred by all these thorns? It seemed impossible. The wall spread for many acres of forest and there seemed to be no end to it.

Red noticed my worried face and exclaimed, "It is an easy obstruction. Beyond this wall are many dangers that you will be up against. It is Water Goblin's protective spell that created this wall. His fear of the wolf family is beyond comprehension to ordinary animals or even humans. Although he knows the wolves can enter this side at any time, he still tries to deter them from doing so. It was only created tonight following a debate that took place after the attack on you. By the way, is there a scar on your face? I heard you were hit."

"No... not any more. Goblin so kindly used a spell to repair the damage caused by the large predator," I explained, touching my cheek.

"His name is Wolfman. If you ever encounter him do not be afraid. He is not what he seems," Red said, in the wolf's defence.

Why would any animal carry a name that includes a reference to the human race? A man was a human being, I contemplated.

"That's a strange name for a wolf. Did he kill a man to be called such a name?" I said, looking down at my sandals.

"It certainly is a strange name. But no, he would not do such a thing. He is of a decent nature, he is a thoughtful individual with intense feelings that only humans have. There—" Red stopped himself as he realised he had said too much. The world was to be kept secret from humans, but now these interferences would definitely expose it.

Red knew that Water Goblin was the one stopping this child from fulfilling her mission. She would have left as soon as she had found what she was looking for. Now that she is here, and such a lovely flower she is, she will evoke humanity in Wolfman. It will be a disaster of wars between the green monster and the forest creatures, an event no soul had ever seen, human or animal. Red had been sent to protect the fragile human being, and he was to ensure she arrived each night at the pond before sunrise. He was to fight with his life to protect hers.

"Would you mind holding me near to the wall, my dear?" Red pleaded.

I did as I was asked and watched Red magically create an opening large enough for me to slip through to the other side. Red circled his paws three times then pointing his right paw, he closed the opening.

"How amazing," I said, in awe.

The other side of the wall was a continuation of the forest, but it looked like a maze. I was surprised that Red knew his way around but then I suppose he was at home. He must know the paths by heart and if he got lost he would use his magic and send himself back to his palace. That last thought made me giggle, which only confused Red.

"With all respect, my dear, would you mind telling me what made you laugh?" Red said.

"I had a thought that triggered this action. My apologies, my friend. I meant no disrespect."

We continued our journey until we arrived at a large plain that seemed to be in the middle of nowhere. It was a large circle of grass. In that circle was an animal, standing still, unmoving. I reckoned by its appearance it could only be a reindeer. As we slowly approached the circle, sending vibrations that travelled to the deer, it lifted its head to look at us.

"We were sent by the Forest Queen. She sends her regards and orders to transport our new friend to any location in order to find an extraordinary flower that has magical powers. The girl has only the night-time to look for it as she is bonded to Water Goblin's orders to return to his palace before sunrise," Red quickly explained to the deer.

It galloped to meet us. Red, being Red, could not help mentioning the earlier attack as well as Goblin's anger which led him to create the wall.

"He had no right to make such an amendment to the forest. Other animals will not be able to move freely, and this will make them angry. The Queen will destroy it before the sun rises," Red explained, now sitting on a branch at my eye level.

The reindeer was enjoying Red's chatter, and several times he gave a strange laugh; it sounded as if he was in pain.

"Here, Joy, this guest is important, her mission must be accomplished." Red finally introduced them. "Joy, meet our guest. What shall we call you? She has no name, not yet."

"How about 'Forest Girl'?" Joy spoke in a manly voice, tender and deep. It echoed in the forests.

"What a brilliant name. It suits her immediate circumstances," Red exclaimed, smiling full-heartedly at me, his cheeks red, and his paws covering his cheeky smile.

I could not complain about my new name; it sounded kind of simple, easy to remember.

Red was not prepared to travel on Joy's back especially after the many times he had fallen off and hurt his paws, tail, and even his tiny ribs had been broken at one time or another. The speed that Joy could break was unbelievable, he could travel as fast as the wind if he wished. Given the circumstances Red had orders to follow and was to be a guard to the Forest Girl at all times. He was not allowed to leave her side as soon as she entered the forests. The Forest Queen must have liked her sweet personality otherwise she would not have shown herself to her. Forest Queen was rarely seen by animals, let alone humans who would have the opportunity to talk to her, he thought to himself.

Red hopped back on to my left shoulder and whispered into my ear, "Hold on tight to his horns, his speed can sway you off his back. If you fall you might get killed."

Joy had massive horns. He must have only been a year or so old as he looked fit and well groomed.

"Sit on my back, Forest Girl, and hold on tight. Red, you had better find a nice, cosy place..." Joy said. "Red's stories about flying with me can be a little bit exaggerated. Don't believe every word he says..." Joy laughed.

His laugh was so loud I had to cover my ears. Red was running like a headless chicken, trying to find a suitable place to sit or hold on to. It seemed he was no longer happy on my shoulder.

"Forest Girl..." He chuckled. "Would I be able to slip into your pocket?" Red asked politely, sitting on Joy's back.

Facing me, he looked so tiny and fragile. I couldn't help wondering how dangerous the ride could be for such a tiny animal.

"Yes, you can," I said.

Her sweet voice travelled slowly into Joy's ear, it was gentle and loving. Joy turned his head just to study Forest Girl's face. He could see she was very young but not yet old enough to marry. What was Green's intention? To keep her that one more year until she matured and marry her? he wondered. If he does that, her soul will be lost forever. Is this the reason why the Forest Queen sent her to him to help in accomplishing her mission? What did they know about this mission? What flower were they to look for?

Joy grew agitated. He did not like the situation that was unfolding before him. They needed to save the Forest Girl before Green got to her entirely. Joy shivered for the first time in many years, but the chill he felt was not due to the cold night.

I offered my right palm to Red. He hopped on, and I placed him gently into my right pocket. Red's head popped out of the pocket, he wiggled his tail for a bit until he found a comfortable way of sitting and held on to the outside of my pocket very tightly with his tiny paws. Red could not get comfortable; there was something in that pocket that was tickling him. He pulled it out.

"A handkerchief? Green's handkerchief!" Red exclaimed in surprise, still holding the handkerchief in his hand. He couldn't believe Forest Girl would have sabotaged them for all the help they had offered her.

"The mission is aborted for tonight, Joy. We will not fly anywhere!" Red said angrily.

As soon as I got off the deer, it took off obediently through the plain and into the other part of the forests. His eyes glinted in the distance as he turned to say goodbye, by lifting his head towards the moon.

"Great!" Red moaned. "This explains the holly tree wall! Green gave you this, did he?" Red said, still angry at the discovery.

"Yes, he gave it to me as protection—" I began to explain.

"It contains spells. When he opens the handkerchief he will see everywhere you have been tonight. I suppose it was given to you after the unexpected attack." Red was not pleased at all. He sounded very disturbed and seemed to be struggling with what to do next.

"Yes, it was. He seemed concerned about the wolf family attacking me again," I said, full of remorse.

"The handkerchief has absorbed every single word and move we have made. It will mirror everything to Green as soon as he gets hold of it. And I am certain he will ask you for it or even take it without you realising."

Red was looking into the handkerchief as if it was an extraordinary item he had never seen before. "We have to see the Forest Queen immediately," he exclaimed and passed me the handkerchief. "Place it back in your pocket, my dear," he said in a much gentler voice now. "She shall reverse the immediate happenings and you will return to Green. You must remember to leave that item at his palace before returning to the forest tomorrow," Red warned.

I was devastated. I had achieved nothing tonight. Even though I had met Joy, he never flew into the air, and I didn't get the chance to tell Red about my vision either. That vision was as clear as it could ever get. I did not even tell him that a flower, the colour of it, had brought about that vision. Now, having achieved nothing, we were going back to where we started, all because of the handkerchief gift. I could kick myself for accepting it.

I walked angrily, unable to understand the consequences the gift could cause if Goblin got hold of it. The many individuals that I would have met along the way would have been chased by an army of Goblin's nasty frogs, and he would not have given up until they had all been killed.

*

Walking back into the forest Red was greatly disappointed but not surprised at Mr Green's actions. The wall that had recently been created had now vanished without trace. Red sat crossly on Forest Girl's shoulder, his arms still locked on his tiny chest. It was not the girl's unawareness of Goblin's craftiness; it was Goblin's tricks that made Red so very cross.

They walked back the right way as if Forest Girl knew the forest like the back of her hand. Red was amazed by her coordination skills but as soon as they reached the area near the pond she became lost. It was only because she did not remember where she had encountered the Forest Queen. Red politely explained the next turn and they moved on vigilantly in case Goblin was lurking somewhere around the pond.

*

I started to recognise that part of the forest. The trees that seemed to touch me with their branches, the movement the trees made as if they were communicating, the familiar wind blowing through the leaves, and then there we were. The massive ancient oak tree stood right in front of us, like the forest was about to end there just like the previous night. It was suddenly in our path. Perhaps it wasn't even there before, but neither of us were looking ahead as we were admiring the communicative trees.

"Hello there, again." The tree spoke softly and kindly as large brown circles appeared in its trunk. The large nose was back in its place, and the mouth with no teeth was talking to them. "What brought you back so early, my dear? Have you found the flower you were looking for?"

"Unfortunately, my Queen, a different set of circumstances has brought us to you." Red jumped in, bowing to the Queen.

"Pleasure to see you, my dear friend Red. What is the matter? And how can I help?" The Queen greeted Red by waving her branches that looked similar to human arms.

"Well, how can I explain this? Well, well, well..." Red struggled to find the right words.

"I accepted a gift from Mr Green," I admitted. "The gift is most probably a record of all my journeys out in the forest. It is a handkerchief that might have absorbed Red's identity as well as Joy's, in which case they will be in danger if Goblin sees them talking to me let alone helping me in my quest," I said softly, full of regret and unable to look at the Forest Queen, knowing I had let everyone down.

"This means we require your extraordinary powers to put everything in order again, my Queen," Red said quietly, with great respect.

"Now, I am not here to blame anyone for this matter. We are encountering an issue that only you, my dear, can solve," the Queen said, pointing at me with her branch hand.

"Yes? How?" I asked, eager to make amends.

"Here is a golden pen and a leaf on which you shall write a note to yourself as a reminder to leave the gift in Green's palace before you arrive here tomorrow. I would advise you to personally return the gift instead of hiding it anywhere in his palace," the Queen instructed.

Suddenly there was a leaf on the floor not far from the Queen's roots and a golden pen. Red hopped down speedily and brought me the tools.

"What..." I stammered.

"Leave the handkerchief at the palace. Love, Red." Red giggled, hiding his little mouth with his paws.

"That is a rather fine message, Red," I said. I wrote down what Red had said jokingly as I knew that was the best way to remind myself not to forget to leave the gift.

"You two are a brilliant team," the Queen said, admiringly. "Now I will reverse everything that happened tonight. The time will set you back to the lovely trunk you sat on earlier. Even though you will not remember what happened tonight you must return to Green's palace. Red will not meet you. You decided to stay in as you feel shaken after the wolf's attack on you..." the

Queen continued, hoping her words would somehow stay with the Forest Girl.

I realised the Forest Queen was observing every movement I made. I knew I was there on that trunk desperately calling Red. Suddenly I started to make things out, although my vision was slightly blurred. Would I remember all these instructions? Then the earth and wind started to take the shape of a hurricane and spun around Red and me. Then the earth stood still.

*

Once again I was sitting on the half trunk, feeling lost. Red was nowhere to be seen. I felt a tremendous need to return to Goblin's palace. Somehow I could not imagine wandering around tonight after the sudden disturbance by the wolf. I stood up then felt something rather large in my pocket. I looked inside the pocket and saw a leaf. How did it get there?

I pulled it out carefully by its stem and to my surprise saw golden paint writing on the leaf. It read: "Leave the handkerchief at the palace. Love, Red".

Was Red here? How did he do that? Why did he require me to leave the gift at the palace? Maybe that was why he was not here tonight. There was something strange about that handkerchief otherwise Red would not go to all that trouble to write this note.

I set off back to the pond to spend the night in Goblin's presence. A very unpleasant thought but there was no alternative. Red would be meeting me tomorrow. Only now I needed to think of an excuse for returning as well as not accepting Goblin's gift which might exasperate him.

I sat at the edge of the pond, my feet immersed in the water, and pondered possible excuses for not needing the quite interesting handkerchief. What a fuss about a gift that was only meant to protect me from evil creatures such as wolves. Maybe I should leave it in this tall grass where no one would ever find it, and even if they did they would hand it to Goblin. At least he would not suspect me of not liking it. Although the note did mention leaving the gift at the palace, there was no way I would be able to find a suitable place to hide it in, or would I? I decided to look for a corner, a tiny gap in a wall where I could leave it, thereby giving Goblin a chance to find it. I still wasn't entirely sure what I was going to do but I swam to the bottom of the pond with it still in my pocket.

The rock to the palace was slightly to the side, so I was able to peek inside, where I saw some twenty to thirty fish at a table that was designed to seat only a few. However, as fish did not require seats, they swam steadily around the table where Goblin sat. This late gathering did not seem to be a "late dinner"; it was a social event, judging by the leaves spread out on the table.

There were leaves from many kinds of trees: oak, beech, alder, silver birch and elm, arranged in rows for each member that was taking part in the game. Not all fish were included as the game was only for six players. Six fish, each with three advisors, against Goblin.

*

Goblin laughed to himself. He knew he would win this game. He would win most of the time, the reason being he cheated, using magic to change his cards frequently to form a set of five cards with different symbols and different pictures. It just would not be the same if Goblin did not cheat; it amused him to see his opposition lose.

The fish looked angry and bothered while Goblin remained cheerful. The advisor fish held leaves in their fins and each advisor fish had one card to hold while the main player fish held two cards. The main player fish had two cards in order to exchange one of them when it was their turn. The fish would firstly dispose of the card it thought was not needed then take a new leaf from the pile. Everyone repeated this over and over again until one of them was holding five different leaves with five different symbols of the moon and five different pictures on them. The game was not as easy as it seemed.

*

I stared in amazement at this strange game taking place before me. As I leaned on the heavy stone the movement sent waves into the palace. Realising my mistake, I walked into the hallway all smiling and innocent-looking, hands clasped behind my back, looking ever so childlike and fragile.

Avoiding the stares of the fish I asked Water Goblin, "Would you mind me asking what you are playing?"

Goblin nearly jumped to his feet but stopped himself. "It is our card night, like many nights, we enjoy playing different games. It is quite a simple game..."

At that, all the fish shook their heads from left to right, disagreeing with their master.

"Well, why don't you join us, and you will see for yourself?" Goblin offered, still sitting, now less afraid of wrongdoing.

"Yes, I would love to try it," I mumbled and walked towards the table.

There was an available chair right next to Goblin so I sat at his right side. Goblin briefly explained the game and let me shuffle the leaves. The leaves were neat, there were many of them and it was rather difficult to shuffle. I dealt the cards. There were 125 cards in total in the deck.

There was a symbol of a full moon with Face of Goblin on an oak leaf, a half-moon facing to the left with the Face of Goblin on an oak leaf, a half-moon facing to the right with the Face of Goblin on an oak leaf, a semi-quarter moon facing to the left with the Face of Goblin on an oak leaf and so on. The game was going to be both entertaining and difficult.

I held my five leaves with pictures facing me in order to hide them from the opposition, but Goblin could see them perfectly. He leaned towards me and whispered, "The full moon with any picture of me are my favourite."

I smiled, only just noticing the symbols on my leaves had suddenly turned into full moons, with different parts of Goblin's body or clothing on different leaves. How was I to make any sense of this? I continued to play the game while watching Goblin from the corner of my eye. I was pretty sure he had not used his magic just yet as he had not won three times in a row since he'd changed my cards. The other fish were delighted though because they were winning. It seemed that Goblin could not stand to lose another game. I noticed sparks and light coming from his fingers.

"Brilllllllliant!" he exclaimed suddenly. Turning towards me, he placed all his leaves on the table with different pictures on them as well as different symbols.

"Congratulations, Mr Green. You are a genius." I giggled as I knew he had cheated to get the right cards.

Goblin laughed too and so did the fish. I could not stop laughing somehow and suddenly I started to cough unexpectedly. I took out the handkerchief given to me by Water Goblin and blew my nose. Goblin eyes widened in disbelief, although he had to admit that a handkerchief was for such a purpose.

I left the handkerchief on the table, and as the evening drew to a close the fish gradually started to leave the table until Goblin and I were the only ones left. I stood up and excused myself, saying I was tired, and went into the bedroom.

*

Goblin sat at the table, open-mouthed, staring at the handkerchief in complete disbelief. His gift had been ruined. He could still retrieve whatever information it held, but he did not feel like doing that any more, considering it had been used.

He got up abruptly and left the palace without a word, taking the handkerchief with him. Although he would not look at it, he placed it in his pocket. It seemed that he would be sleeping every night behind the tall grass under the blue skies, as his occupant was taking up his weedy bed. He was tired now, recalling the games from earlier and all the players' stunned faces when he won a couple of games in a row, and on that thought he fell asleep.

8

The Ride

A man sat at a wooden table in a house made from wood. A boy with blonde hair paced up and down in the room where the man sat. The man stared at the door in front of him, undisturbed by the boy's pacing. His expression was blank. The boy scratched his chin then stroked it. He lifted his head up then hung it back low again.

*

I opened my eyes to see Water Goblin walking into the bedroom. I rubbed my eyes, the picture of the man and the boy fading away. Goblin was moving around the room. Deep in thought, he picked up some clothes, pulled out secret drawers and rummaged through them. What is he looking for? Why is he looking for it now?

I sat up. "Would you mind telling me what you are looking for?"

Goblin did not answer. He left the room, his head low, staring at his feet and not even taking the slightest peek at me. I yawned, lay back down and closed my eyes. What did I experience in the forest last night? Why didn't Red meet me? The game last night, that was something different, oh, how good. I left the handkerchief on the table. Dropping into a deep sleep I lay on the bed lifeless.

*

A wolf ran towards me. I stood motionless, but my hands began to shake and my knees began to give away. I could hear my breath and I covered my mouth with my hands. The predator charged towards me and knocked me to the ground, though the ground felt soft, very soft. It placed its front paws on my shoulders, and staring at me, licked my face. I looked at the monster, at its large jaw and ugly set of teeth that could at any second tear my face apart. I looked into its eyes again and did not leave its gaze.

*

My eyes flew open. I was lying on the weedy bed.

"The animal," I cried. "The animal had human eyes," I wailed into the empty bedroom, gasping for air. I jumped up. I hugged my stomach, the prickles in the pit of it now faded away.

Goblin was not aware that the spells were not strong enough to affect the girl during the period of sleep, and the spells were gradually wearing off because of her motivation to discover her real purpose of coming to the forests.

Was it possible that an animal could be a human at the same time? No, it couldn't be, could it?

I wiped my face, my closed eyes absorbing the darkness. I shivered, opened my eyes and looked around the room. I moved towards the walls, and my hand caressed the unevenness of the mud structure. Years breathed through them. Where were those drawers? Would I be able to open them and look inside? I checked every inch of the walls but my hand stayed clean, no moss or other underwater creatures, not even on the shelf where a glass jar stood. The place was immaculate and still. The silence was deafening. I spotted a little fish, so tiny it could swim through the tiniest gaps in the walls, not that there were any visible anywhere. It swam in through a gap where the boulder had left cracks in the walls. Fish were forbidden from entering Goblin's palace unless he was present.

I lay flat on my back again, the soft cushion of weeds engulfing my body. I was not going back to sleep again. I was waiting for Goblin to allow me out any minute now.

Goblin walked in and I sat up on the bed. My long hair hung loose and reached my waist. Goblin's mouth opened, staring at the length of my silky brown hair. He was used to my hair always being in a ponytail. His own green hair was scarce and dry like sand on a sunny day. Over the years the pond's water changed its colour, texture and length. Goblin's hair reached his shoulders and when dried in the sun it shrunk in length by nearly a half.

I cradled my hair in my palms, ran my fingers through my hair and secured it back into a ponytail. The ogling Goblin prevented me from plaiting it. This strange creature took away my freedom, he dominated my whereabouts. There was nothing else I wanted more than to know who I was before I entered the green water that is now my home.

Goblin shook his head, closed his eyes then opened them again. "I fetched the fireflies l-last night. Would you like to hel-lp me tonight?"

I nodded and he indicated for me to hold the jars he began placing in my arms. I followed Goblin out of the palace. We emerged at the banks of the pond. A jar became loose and I stretched out my right arm to catch it. Goblin reached out at the same time and grabbed it. He placed it beside him on the ground then picked the rest of the jars.

"It is not as easy as it looks." He held out his arm to help me out of the pond, and I reached for it.

"Thank you. It seems an easy chore when you swim unaided holding the jars."

We entered the forest.

"I have had many days of practice, my little friend."

I covered my wide smile with my hands. Mr Green, with a jar and a lid in his hands, stretched his arms and hopped on one leg but the fireflies flew away just as he was about to snap the lid on them. He swayed from side to side again, extended his arms and trapped one firefly.

I clapped loudly, still smiling. "Well done..."

He bent down, grabbed an empty jar and a lid and passed it to me. "It's your turn. It's very simple..."

My mouth went dry. I looked at the objects in my hands. Am I to run around like a headless chicken catching fireflies? Would I be able to catch even one? I gently lifted the jar with my right arm above my head. Fireflies flew madly and I watched them, waiting patiently. My eyes opened wide, my jaw dropped. A firefly flew into the jar and sat on the glass wall.

"Ouch," I heard a very tiny voice say.

Goblin frowned, his eyes opened wide. "Wow. It appears catching insects comes naturally to you."

I moved my arms gently so that the jar was at the level of my waist and placed the corresponding lid on to close the jar. The firefly sat there in the same position, as if it had done this all before. I brought the jar closer to my face and stared at the tiny bug. It winked at me.

Goblin took his hat off and clapped. "Wow." He could not understand how this stranger to the forest was able to perform this task with such ease. The animals loved her, they adored her, they liked her more than me, he admitted to himself. Why? Is it because I am unnaturally green? Some animals' colouring was not better than mine, so what was this? A conspiracy against me or just one-time luck?

Goblin's smile turned to a frown. Animals seemed to be taking to the human being easier than to the forest's more permanent occupant. Never mind, she is a naturally likeable person. It may be a good thing after all. His smile returned, although the corner of his mouth indicated mischief.

Once we had caught all fourteen fireflies we returned to the palace. I placed the last jar on a shelf in the bedroom. Goblin turned to me in the doorway.

"If you would like to stay, we will be playing another game tonight. In a few moons' time we will be playing other games that may be of interest to you, my dear."

I played with my dress, watching it crease in my fingers. "I will certainly join you for another game some other time. Today I just wish to explore the outside forest, if you don't mind."

"Yes, of course, of course."

With that Goblin turned away, and I left quickly.

*

At the forest I met Red who started on me immediately.

"Have you done what was written on the note?"

I offered my left palm to him, but he remained sitting on a tree branch.

"Yes, I did. I left the article on the table last night as we played Mr Green's famous game of cards. Very interesting game we played, I must say." I giggled when I talked about Goblin's cheating throughout the games, to which the fish were totally oblivious. Why was that? I did not know.

Red paced up and down the branch, arms held behind his back. "Would you be so kind as to check your pockets, my dear child, just in case he could have placed it there?" Red stopped pacing.

"No, I don't mind, my friend." I checked my pockets and turned them inside out.

There was nothing in my dress pockets which satisfied Red. He jumped on my left shoulder and sang:

"First ride on the Reindeer

Only animals could fear

Falling off the fast male

Fatal injuries are not rare

The trip is never mundane."

We walked on, chatting happily about the forest animals and their behaviour, and of course Red's adventures which was the main topic of our conversation. We passed the place where the wall of holly trees had stood the previous night. Red expected me to ask many questions, why and how it had disappeared but then realised I had no recollection of last night as all events had been undone.

He was only aware of the events that happened due to the magical powers he possessed. He enjoyed extraordinary abilities including past vision, mind-reading, to mention a few. Being a tiny creature, he already had plenty of advantages like moving fast and being able to hide in the tiniest of places. He considered himself blessed already, even more so because of his extraordinary powers.

Red sat on my shoulder with his arms folded. His expression was one of pure contentment.

It feels good to help others, I am glad I was required. I hope I can show my abilities, my powers to the girl, he thought to himself.

We arrived at the plain where we met Joy again.

Joy bowed his head, his mighty antlers moved towards me. "Nice to meet you. I am Joy."

I smiled. "You too."

Red stroked his chin and stared into the distance as he mused to himself, I am one of the only creatures who knows what happened last night. I am lucky to have that advantage, and obviously the Forest Queen who is the instigator of the spell. Hmmm... nice. I am one step ahead of many creatures, even the fastest animal of the whole forest grounds. Though with extra powers come extra responsibilities, so in this case I am responsible for my little forest friend.

Joy came closer and lifted his head towards Red. "What are you up to?"

Red backed away and leaned closer into my neck. "I am... I am thinking of a name... Would 'Forest Girl' be ok? What do you think?" He patted me on my cheek.

Joy opened his mouth then closed it again. Joy's eyes were pinned on Red, as he said, "Very suitable name." Joy was convinced Red had used his advantages over him and stole his thought to impress the girl.

Red's eyes thinned to grains of rice through which he gazed at Joy. The events must fall into each other as they were meant to, Red thought.

I broke the silence. "May I?"

Joy positioned himself closer to me. "Of course."

Red ran down my back and climbed into my right pocket. I leapt on to Joy's back with my companion, Red, settled in my pocket.

"It will be an experience of a lifetime. By using Joy's ability to fly we will be able to cover a vast amount of land in a shorter period of time," Red said, excitedly.

I looked down at Red. "It is yellow, bright yellow. Its stem and leaves are yellow, and the petals are bluish-greenish colour. We can't miss it. It's extraordinary—"

Red interrupted. "What is it?"

My eyes widened. "It's the flower. It's a medicine that will help someone..."

Now that she knew exactly what we are looking for it will be easier to concentrate on the search for it, Red thought. He had expected happiness to be radiating out from her but there was only that instance of surprise. There must have been a lot more than just a spell used to keep this girl underwater, but what did that Green creature do? What did he do to achieve that obedience?

Joy turned his head to us as much as he could. "Now off we go to find the flower. We will fly at slow speed, so do not panic, and at times at low altitude to make sure you find that which you are looking for."

I swayed slightly from side to side and I tightened my grip on Joy's horns. I am sure Joy would not speed up recklessly, leaving me hanging on to his horns for dear life. The speed he travelled at was steady. The tops of the leafy trees were below us, and we began to see the vast amount of forest, mountains spreading for many miles and countless trees that anyone could get lost in for several days.

*

Mr Green shivered. What if the girl breaks the spell? I can't lose my companion, my captured prey. I have no knowledge of where my guest is during the nights although I am certain that as long as I am in possession of her heart she would not be able to live an ordinary human life. Therefore, she would always return to me. He caressed the tall grass with his fingers then pulled up a handful. I have that most precious article of human nature, but I do not understand why she returned my gift last night.

The event unfolded too fast for him to recollect. He saw the girl placing it on the table, he knew she had wiped her nose with it. He shook his head and panted. He pulled out the handkerchief from his pocket and looked into it as if he wanted to see himself in it.

"Bother!"

There was the girl sitting on a trunk, then there was him and the fish at his table playing cards.

"That's it?" he stammered.

The handkerchief was to protect her from evil predators that might have preyed on her. It would have mirrored events to him, places and animals she had met during her walkabouts. Now I am unable to see what my guest gets up to. I must find a different way to guard her, to spy on her better. I will not take any more chances of losing her because next year I will marry her.

He sat outside the pond at his favourite spot. "Ha ha ..." he roared into the empty air. "Ha ha ha ..." echoed into the woods. It must have reached the girl's ears, I am certain of it. She is my possession, she should know she cannot go too far for me to not reach her. I am Goblin after all. I possess powers. My army of frogs, mosquitoes and other insects can be ready at the click of my fingers.

"Ha ha ha..." echoed into the distance again.

Devious Mr Green lay in his usual spot and stared at the sky which was rather well populated with stars as well as the full moon that had reigned in the sky for the last few days.

"Bright sky, bright sky
Will bring much delight
To everyone that looks at it
Will enjoy the sight of it
All through the night."

The wall he had created only the night before had been destroyed by the Queen as soon as she had learned of its existence from her trusted guards. He knew it would not last a second, but he'd still had a go at making it. His guest had not even noticed its sudden appearance as she spent the night playing cards with him.

*

I pointed at a plain where flowers grew.

"Look, Red, we could see if the flower might be there. Isn't the view beautiful?"

Although there were many flowers about, most closed themselves for the night.

Red shouted towards me, "Joy flies nightly over these grounds. He knows every corner of the forests as well as the mountains."

I nodded in Red's direction and then faced him. He seemed nice and cosy in my pocket. "Pardon me, my dear friend?" I placed my hands on Joy's antlers. Red deflated like a popped balloon. The howling of wolves persisted in the distance. As it was night they were preparing for mischief as well as preying on potential dinner.

Joy turned his head slightly. "We will be landing soon."

We landed on a plain somewhere between two mountains. I climbed down from Joy's back and found my legs immersed in the green cushion of knee-high grass. The howling of wolves was relatively louder on this side, and I looked around me rather vigilantly. I will put up a fight this time if I am attacked by such a wild creature, I told myself.

Red shook his head, thinking to himself, I am not sure Forest Girl will like the next step of the journey, but unfortunately it is a necessary piece of the puzzle that surrounds her.

Red jumped out of my pocket and climbed on to my left shoulder. "Forest Girl, follow me." He leapt into the air and landed on a nearby branch.

I followed him into the forest. Where am I heading? North, west, south, east? It doesn't matter what direction I am going in as I have no idea where I am anyway.

Red jumped from one branch to another. "Can you see me, Forest Girl?" he shouted.

I nodded.

A dark blanket engulfed the forest, but Red could see the path clearly.

A branch hit my face, I pushed it away. It was an endless repetition. I stepped on a tree root and spread my arms on my sides balancing my body. "Ouch... prrrr..." I swept branches away from my face and pulled my legs free from brambles. Red is so tiny we might lose him and become trapped in these never-ending mountains. Oh, the fireflies were back. They were flying above my head again, lighting my passage.

Red stopped and indicated for me to be still. His eyes sparkled in the dark. Trees around us stood like spies, here and there. We were standing in front of a patch of dried soil with an opening to the ground: an animal's den. I could enter it without difficulty. The darkness of the night resembled the entrance. Red jumped up and down, a tiny glass tube in his paw. "Hurray," he said, lifting the tube towards me. My eyes opened wider and I covered my mouth. A firefly lit my face. Why didn't we do that a long time ago?

Holding the tube, he gestured me to squat and faced me. "No need to worry, Forest Girl. Do not be frightened of what you will experience now." I nodded. Red turned around and shed some light into the den. He walked in, calling loudly, "Come out, you all!"

Who did we need on this quest? Who else was to come with us? The journey was becoming rather interesting; meeting strange talking and flying animals was not everyone's dream. Four large male wolves approached Red, their fur long, their eyes pinned on him. They circled him, eyeing him like prey.

Red shouted, holding the tube high and in their faces, lighting up the four angry animals. "Be not afraid, Forest Girl."

I raised my eyebrows. Red was so tiny he could barely cover my foot let alone protect my whole being. Although the way he was standing in front of me was sending a message to the wolves to not even dare look at me. More and more wolves emerged from the dark den. Four females emerged with countless cubs tumbling around their legs.

I walked forward and scooped up Red into my palms. He turned around to fight off whatever was holding him. He shook his head at me as I brought him towards my face.

"Forest Girl," he gasped. "The cubs are very playful."

A female wolf stepped forward from the group. "Welcome, Red, my squirrel friend. How are you doing?" Her voice was friendly. "What a pleasant surprise. You brought with you the person every animal is talking about. May I say, my dear, you are welcome here too."

The wolf smiled, watching me.

"My name is Sef and I am the leader of this group. There are many wolf families about. Our group consists of twelve males, eleven females and countless cubs. We reside in this part of the forest and are the largest pack in the surrounding mountains."

She moved towards me and I instinctively backed away.

"You are safe with our pack. If you ever encounter other packs just mention you are friends with Sef's lot and not one wolf will attack you."

The wolves and their cubs sat in a circle, including me with Red on my lap. Sef's friendly talks continued for several hours. She told us about places in the forest that not many animals knew about. Sef mentioned adventures spent hunting for food, chasing crafty foxes and playing in the river.

I poked Red who climbed on to my shoulder. I turned towards him and whispered. "It is the key to our next step. The flower."

Red nodded.

Sef's eyes found mine. "The many wolves that went hunting for prey tonight will be returning soon. I can smell their presence now. They are a friendly lot, so don't worry." She directed that last bit towards me as she stared above my head. I spun round to see what she was looking at and Red lost his balance, ending up in my lap.

I saw a massive wolf, much larger than the rest of the flock. It placed its right paw on my left shoulder.

"I did not expect any guests tonight, Sef. Whom did the wind bring to us?" the wolf enquired harshly then shouted, "Red, my friend..."

Red offered his tiny paw to the wolf who took it and shook it eagerly, making Red sway from side to side.

The wolf showed his teeth. "Oh, sorry, my friend. I always forget you are so very small. Hahahaha."

They roared into the forests, but I stood there watching them with my mouth open. There, shaking Red's hand was my attacker, the predator who had knocked me down on to the bare soil while all the animals had watched in horror. Now, here I was, face to face with the beast whose body structure was larger than the common wolf. Surely he would not attack me again in the presence of his fellow wolves, especially as I was a friend of Red's?

The wolf put his paw back on the ground. "Well, well, my friend. You have travelled far to meet us. What is it that we can help you with?"

Red ran on to the wolf's back and began to explain. "It's common knowledge that a girl has been captured by Green and he wishes to keep her for eternity. She is not from our world and being a human, she would not be able to survive in the forests. The Forest Queen," – at this, everyone facing Red bowed their heads – "has gathered many of her best and various in order to help this child to find the thing she came to find. The mission is not as simple as it sounds. The girl only remembers so much, in particular she has a recollection of a flower as bright as the sun with petals of bluish and greenish colour. We have no idea where the flower grows and what the flower is to be used for. Green has taken Forest Girl's memory, and that is about all we know. The sacrifice made to be able to live underwater must have been great, but that shall be our secondary concern."

The wolf turned towards Red. "I like the name you have given her."

"Forest Girl was Joy's original idea..." Red mumbled.

Mumbling spread across the crowd. Wolf and Red walked towards me. I sat on a stone near the meeting. I was not listening to Red's speech as I was rather preoccupied by two tiny wolves that had snuggled in my lap.

"Oh dear. Asleep, are they?" Red noted.

But Wolf roared, "Move, you two!" He waited till they had run off. "They are hunters, do not baby them!"

I hung my head. I was only being kind to them.

Red scurried from the wolf's back to his head. "Well, meet Wolfman, my dear. This is his soft side, he can be rather serious towards everyone..."

I looked up, my teeth gritted and my lips thin. "It seems that you are excluded from the group of everyone, dear Red."

"We are old pals," Wolfman snapped.

I offered my hand but Wolfman did not shake it. "Forest Girl," I said. I brought my arm back close to my body. "Mr Wolfman, I believe we have already met."

Red sat on Wolfman's head, crossed his legs and supported his chin with one of his palms. Wolfman lifted his head and sent Red toppling over on his back.

"Yes, we have. My warning to you was delivered and a warning to Mr Green as well. You are in danger, the extent of which you have no idea. Water Goblin is a crafty old—" Wolfman stopped when he saw me holding out my arms to Red. Wolfman stood on his hind legs and grabbed my shoulders with his front paws. "You will die, girl! Be afraid!"

Red curled into a ball and rolled to the ground. My hair blew away from my face, although not one muscle moved on my face. He lifted my body into the air, but my eyes never left his face.

Placing me back on the ground, Wolfman walked towards Red who patted his fur. Wolfman's head hung low, his eyes fixed on the ground. "She has no feelings. She may seem normal at times, acts normal only due to her brain functioning. She is able to reason but unable to feel!"

I sat on a nearby stone as Wolfman and Red discussed the unusual discovery.

Red climbed back on to the wolf. "Another obstacle. Green would not make it easy, would he?"

"That's for sure!" Wolfman walked towards the other wolves with Red still on his back while cubs gathered around me again.

I talked to Sef and the other females in the pack. Sef sensed something and turned around. Seeing it was only Joy, she relaxed.

Joy kept his distance as he said, "I apologise for this uninvited disturbance. Unfortunately, the night is coming to an end and therefore I advise that we transport Forest Girl back to Green's."

This flying creature had attracted everyone's attention. Cubs began to gather around his legs. "Can we have a ride? Please, please, Uncle Joy...?"

Joy backed away. He lifted one cub by his mouth and placed it away from his hooves. He had to repeat this a few times. "No, no, no... not now, little ones."

Wolfman moved forward to help the poor deer. "Here we go, Joy. You are very popular around here." He moved some cubs away and Red hopped on them until he reached Joy.

Joy retorted, "Seems you don't like my presence around your lot."

Wolfman defended himself. "None are mine, but all are my brothers and sisters in heart."

"Well, we heard you are a different breed..." Joy turned his head sharply towards me. Our eyes met and I swam in those brown circles for a minute.

Red waved at me. He sat on Joy's back. "Joy, we are ready to go any time you're ready, my outspoken friend."

Laughter echoed into the distance. Red and I settled on the deer, waved towards the pack and took off into the cold night.

DANIELA BURLEY

9

The Flower

Wolfman sat on a lonely patch of grass, surrounded by his companions: trees, standing like soldiers, ready to attack. His eyes glinted in the moonlight. Scenes replayed in his mind like a song on repeat. Something had happened on that particular spot many years ago. Wolfman knew that event from Sef who had brought him up; she was his mother. He frowned, threw his head back and howled into the night. He jumped on to all four paws, lifted his front right leg and howled for a bit longer. His body collapsed on the ground, weak as if he had been beaten by hundreds of wolves.

I won't raise my paw against a defenceless animal, I can't kill like my brothers do. I am not like them and I never will be. What is the use of this big build if unless I am attacked I won't attack others, and I won't feed on other animals, or humans for that matter, unless I have to? On many occasions I have led the night hunting group, and those same times I disappeared off the earth only to appear on the group's return, when they carried plenty of food to eat. The wolves thought I was the leader therefore there was no need for me to catch prey, which was very convenient for me.

Tonight, Wolfman didn't have a chance to spend any time with Forest Girl and enquire about her being in the forest. Red had given him some information, however. Wolfman got up, howled then walked away.

He arrived at an ancient tree and bowed. "My dear Forest Queen, I have come to ask…"

The Queen opened her eyes. "Hello, Wolfman. I know what brings you here. You are strong in every way to solve this. I would like you to look after the girl. I see trouble ahead." She waved her branch arm at him. Sparkles hit Wolfman whose head was still bent low. He lifted his head and their eyes met. "Do not forget where she came from or belongs to. Do not get carried away and do not jump to conclusions, dear friend Wolfman," the Queen warned.

Wolfman silently considered the situation he found himself in. I can nail this one easily, it is a piece of cake. It's not as if I have an army to fight, although the Forest Queen did warn this could happen. Someone must be missing their daughter by now? Did she have parents? Was she abandoned like me? No, I cannot go there, I cannot start thinking of myself and feeling sorry for myself while a human needs my helping paw. He shook his head vigorously for some time.

Before the night turned to dawn, Wolfman returned to the den where all the wolves greeted him gratefully. He was their power, his enormous body was their shield, not that any of them should be afraid of other animals. He was an idol to the cubs, a hero to the older wolves and a good listener to the female wolves, although never attached to any of them. He was like them but not of them.

*

Green's fish swam about the front room and some secret cupboards. Before they began their usual shift Mr Green stopped them.

"Do not awaken my guest, otherwise I shall have you for dinner tonight."

Some fish bit at the soil, other fish moved their tails up and down on the floor. They moved bits of soil from the palace out to the lake. The third lot of fish munched on grass growing around the palace.

*

I opened my eyes and looked around the room. I lay in the bed, engulfed by seaweeds. The walkway into the room was as bare as the night sky without the moon. My eyes moved back to the ceiling. Sound in my ears repeated from last night. Why would Mr Green want to cause me any harm? Maybe he is lonely in his shady old palace, keen for me to stay. I placed my right index finger on my lips. Where would we sleep? Now, I was occupying his bed which was only large enough for one being. Mr Green would not sleep night after night under the open skies. One night it will rain, and when winter arrives he will need his bed back. Would he then abandon me in the forests? I sat up. Who is he? Why does he want me to stay here when the palace is meant for one person? Why...

Goblin walked into the room and I turned my head towards him. A large carp swam beside him, moving his tail from side to side. They sat at the table where they had played Goblin's card games two nights ago. Goblin poured sand from one of his glass jars on to the large table. The carp swam about the top of the table scribbling lines and shapes of some kind. I turned my body to the left and swung my legs round to the floor, my eyes pinned on the two strangers working together on some unusual project. Should I join them?

I raised my arm then let it gently lower down. "Hello there."

Water Goblin faced me, his eyes wide open. He lifted his right arm up as if to wave. "Good evening, my dear. Above the pond a table has been set up for you to enjoy some food. The frogs are at your service."

I heard my stomach rumble, and with both hands I squeezed it. "Oh, thank you so much."

Above the palace I sat at the boulder we had used for the feast only recently. Frogs sat beside me, opposite me, on the boulder and on the grass. A line of frogs walked from one end of the boulder towards me. They placed leaves of fruits, nuts and larvae in front of me. Larvae appeared to be a special dish. I had no choice but to eat such food, so I tucked into it. The frogs opposite watched me placing the food in my mouth. I chewed it but their eyes were glued on me, staring, observing and gawking. I looked at them. Oh, I hope it is soon time to walk away into the forest for another adventure but not right now, the frogs would certainly follow me. They seemed pretty nosy for ordinary water creatures. Their behaviour and their features had something to do with Mr Green, I am certain of that. He is using spells to fortify these little defenceless creatures. Is it the attack that's making him cautious and driving him towards using tricks?

Goblin placed his hand on my left shoulder. I resisted turning my head round to face him.

"Did you enjoy your dinner, my friend?" he said, seeing the leaves on the table, most of which were empty.

"Yes, thank you, Mr Green."

Goblin looked around. The boulder was exposed to any creature. A picture of the girl sitting at the table facing wide grassy open space stayed in his mind. Grass. That will not protect my guest or... he smirked, myself from Wolfman or, or any other creature! This is not an appropriate place to dine on a daily basis, he decided. He turned his head from side to side, his eyes scanning the plain. They stopped at the old willow, and he pictured him and his guest enjoying a meal together in peace. "That's the place," he mumbled.

Goblin offered his hand to help me up. "You may go to the forest now, and if you wish I will walk with you. When you return, there may be a surprise waiting for you."

I took his hand and with his help stood up. "It will not be necessary," I said, averting his gazing eyes. "I will find my way. It is my nightly experience discovering every corner of the surrounding forests."

"I am glad that is what interests you. You—" Green stopped himself from interrogating the girl about her nightly whereabouts.

She is my guest not my wife, not yet anyway, he reminded himself with a smirk. She will be the prettiest bride in the green pond.

I wandered away into the forest leaving Green to his mischievous thoughts, not knowing that his intentions gave him a great advantage over me. The moon lit up the sky, shining plenty of light over my path. I heard the wolves howling in the far distance, probably attracted to the bright moonlight. Their howling set a trail of thoughts in my mind. I was attacked by Wolfman, who apparently was a close friend of my friend Red. Incredible circumstances. Supposedly he was only warning me as well as Mr Green of his presence, of him being on Green's case. What warning was he transferring to me then? Warning me that Mr Green would keep me imprisoned for eternity if I did not follow Wolfman's orders? Who was he to be trusted? He will need to prove his innocence and that his attack on me was only to warn me or my master. My master? My master has a surprise for me when I return at sunrise; that is, if I return. What would Mr Green do if I did not, if I sneaked into the village instead? Foxes knew the village well; they stole glass jars from around there as well as preyed on the chickens. Would he chase after me? Would his anger be beyond human comprehension?

*

Red sat on a branch, his eyes pinned on the girl.

I walked towards the tree he was in, oblivious to his presence. He leapt into the air and landed on a branch of the next tree I would pass. I turned my head in his direction and stretched out my left arm. He hopped on to my palm, and I placed him on my shoulder. He opened his mouth, closed it then opened it again, scratching his chin.

"Wolfman has to devise a plan to access Green's trustees one of these days in order to retrieve some information about your ability to live underwater. As we know, humans are only able to swim and would drown if they stayed underwater for too long," Red said.

I turned my head slightly to the right. My left ear came closer to Red. All the powers the forest possessed but never showed to the human eye were interesting. How much information did I have to contribute to find out the real me and the real reason I lost my way in the forest? I stopped walking.

"It is all so confusing. Wolfman will have no access to any of Mr Green's trustees due to his earlier attack on Green's palace. No one would trust a wolf after experiencing such a wild disturbance."

We sat on a damp patch of grass and waited for Joy.

Red pulled a face. "He will not be able to go himself. He definitely has a plan for me to accomplish. It sure will be hard. I would only do it for you, Forest Girl." He pushed against my right arm with his left paw.

I smiled, nodding in an agreement. "You have a heart."

"Really?" Red said in mock surprise then giggled. "I try—"

Joy appeared and we set off above the many trees into the far distance until we arrived somewhere at a mountain where Wolfman was already waiting for us.

He greeted us. "I have been searching around for a flower that was described to me by Red. I will be taking you to the place that is only accessible by road. Joy has done his job for now. He will wait for us at this spot."

He started to describe his plan, showing us he had the situation under control. Red and I watched him, our eyes meeting. Wolfman walked closer to us.

"It will be easier for you to jump on me with Red. It will take half a night to get there if we walk."

"Yes, sir. To your command." I then whispered to Red, "Are we safe riding on a wolf?"

"Oh, yes. He rides carefully, and if he has you to look after he will be even more careful." Red reminded me they were all here to help me.

All this hassle for me, and I don't even know why I need this flower. "Red, what will happen after we find the flower? I am not even sure why I need it, although I know it is a cure..."

Red moved his hand about as he spoke. "Once the flower is found, and it is the right one, it must bring some recollection to you. From that point we will progress to the next step in Wolfman's plan. But until we find the flower we are unable to move forward."

I leapt on Wolfman daringly with Red in my pocket. I gripped the long fur around Wolfman's neck and off we went racing against the wind. Trees passed by speedily while I visually scanned the area. A pine needle carpet covered the mountain we were on. I pressed my body close to the wolf's soft fur and kept my head turned to the right. The fresh night air hit my left cheek.

Small animals scurried amongst the many trees: rabbits, foxes and wolves. The sound of owls hooting could be heard from time to time. Wolfman's legs burrowed in small bushes that bore blueberries in the summer. He climbed a steep hill with ease; the endless grass that would not reach my knees if I were to stand in the forest spread. The mountain stood high, and the steeper we climbed the quicker the temperature began to drop. Hopefully Wolfman had not found the flower at the very peak of the mountain, not that I was feeling the chill; it was Red who was wriggling around in my pocket.

"Red, what is the matter?"

He popped his head out of my dress pocket. "I am warming myself up. It's nearly freezing, Forest Girl. Movement will send my blood rushing around my body and warm me up."

We could barely hear each other but this did not discourage us. We approached a plain covered by green grass except for a little stream of pure blue water, which sailed over the rocks creating a line as wide as a quarter of a human's body. There were blueberry bushes all around, amongst some tall grass that came up to my waist.

I got off the monstrous wolf. It stood next to me, not facing me but looking thoughtfully around.

"You stay here!"

I nodded. It was an order, and orders were to be obeyed as far as I was concerned. I grew up in the village where orders were enforced by the ministry of Galonia.

Wolfman took step after step, his back low like a hunter waiting to pounce on its prey, his ears moved towards any noise he heard. I wondered what Wolfman was up to. I didn't think he was particularly hungry. Perhaps he was making sure there were no other large predators lying in wait. Wolfman disappeared for a while, during which time Red and I stood in silence, frozen to the spot. Surely Wolfman would come back soon.

Suddenly, Wolfman reappeared from behind me.

"It's all clear," he said.

I jumped, nearly dropping Red who was curled up in my palms. I turned towards Wolfman, and Red jumped on to a branch. I flung my arms in the air and clenched my fists. "That was pretty unfair!"

Wolfman brought his right paw towards his mouth but it did not cover his grin. "Just checking that you are paying attention."

Red laughed. "You will get used to his sense of humour."

With my fists still clenched, I faced Red. "It seems you, Red, are not used to his sense of humour just yet and you have known him for many years."

Red licked his lips to disguise the ever-evident smile. "Well, I did not expect him to do such a thing to you to." His teeth appeared, his eyes glinted. "It is only a friendly gesture."

My fingers began to stretch, my shoulders relaxed. "Possibly…"

Out of the corner of my eye a large brown bear visualised, approaching us steadily from behind Wolfman.

Wolfman lifted his head up towards us. "I found it."

I grabbed Wolfman by its ear as if in revenge, turned his head and then pointed at the approaching predator.

"Oh dear. It's Brown Bear. No need to be frightened of him."

Wolfman had a feeling he'd now scored twice in a row with this one small joke. I let go of his ear, and he rubbed it gently.

"Brown Bear is a trusted friend of mine."

I took a deep breath and stumped my foot. "Nice to know!"

Wolfman stopped rubbing his ear and wiped his mouth with the back of his paw. "That hurts, by the way, girl!" His belly contracted as if he was going to vomit, but in his case the contraction was caused by him holding his laugh.

Red sat silent on my left shoulder. He did not take sides. It seems the two are getting to know each other, Red thought to himself.

Wolfman pointed at the bear. "Brown Bear will lead us to the special flower."

I swirled my lips. "Well, let him lead us."

Red patted me on the cheek. "Forest Girl, let me introduce another member of the team that shall help us in our search: Brown Bear."

The large bear wobbled towards me and shook my tiny right hand with his extra-large paw.

"It is a pleasure to meet you, Forest Girl." He had a very deep voice, rather appropriate for his tall and chubby build.

"Nice to meet you, Brown."

Once the introductions were out of the way we followed the large furry animal called Brown.

Brown turned to Red and me. "Red, you want to hop on my shoulder?" Red looked at me as Brown added, "My fur will protect you from the chill, my friend."

Red shuffled his bottom and placed his paw under his chin. Wolfman caught up with us and gestured to Red that it would be a good idea for him to hop on to Brown's shoulder. It seemed Brown had something to discuss.

Red turned to me. "Excuse me, my friend." Then he hopped on to Brown's right shoulder. My eyes followed Red and I smiled.

Wolfman matched my step and we walked quietly behind the Brown–Red team. I kept imagining the flower. What if Wolfman had seen it? I lifted my right arm and faced the wolf beside me.

"May I ask you if you have seen the flower yourself?"

Wolfman answered, "The item you are looking for had been described to me rather precisely. This information was then passed to Brown who consulted his helpers to search for the special specimen."

I threw my hands into the air. "I just... I wanted you to tell me its visual features and colours. Never mind, we shall be seeing it very shortly."

We heard mumbling but could not make out the words. The gap between Red, Brown and us got wider. Wolfman and I sped up.

Brown pushed a branch away from Red. "Once the girl sees the flower, her memory will flood back. However, we are not sure her feelings will return. Once her memory comes back, her behaviour will change. She cannot let the Goblin know, and the flower cannot be taken until she becomes human again. Her reptile abilities and inhumanity will be recognised by the humans immediately. The flower has to be preserved once it has been disconnected from its source of life. It is then to be used within one moon's change as a medicine to heal magically. Whoever is in need of that medicine has been exposed to our world. The medication only lasts for one year before it wears off." Red patted Brown's shoulder. "Our mission has not been accomplished just yet. The girl has no feelings, and they might not return even if the flower is the right one. We need to find out how Water Goblin achieved that. After her experience she might have the answer. She must have seen what happened to her under the water when he pulled her in."

We walked for a while longer. The hill we were climbing became gradually steeper. Large stones poked out of the ground amongst short grass and flowers of various kinds. Blueberry bushes and a sea of green grass polluted another plain we stepped into. Above the plain amongst rocks from beneath the ground a stream surged. A stripe of yellow colour beamed at us from amid the grass. Brown did not stop Wolfman and me from going forward.

My eyes were drawn to the yellow stripe. I walked past Brown and headed for the source of this bright colour. A flower with a yellow stem, yellow leaves and half bluish, half greenish petals stood there. Stinging nettles surrounded it like hyenas circle their prey. It stood there in its full glory, oblivious of its importance to me. Its petals would tickle my knees if the stinging guards would allow me to get closer. I stretched out my arm and opened my palm above it. Its head fit my palm and reflected greenish blueish colours on to it.

Red hopped impatiently on Brown's back. It was right there in front of us, the miraculous flower I needed. Wolfman hurried forward, the yellow colour mirrored in his eyes. He stopped beside me, turned his head towards me, his mouth open and his eyes wide.

"Don't do it, Forest Girl," Wolfman warned.

The words echoed in my ears. I continued to stare at the bright yellow stomp while pictures of me, my father and my mother ran across my mind. I dropped to my knees and placed my face in the palms of my hands. I saw my mother bringing that exact flower and making a special tea out of it. I saw my father drinking the tea that night. I was eight when I realised my father was unable to talk or move like ordinary people. It was the first and the last time I saw that strange flower. Since then Ma wandered endlessly around the forests searching for that flower. She always returned empty-handed due to not being able to walk too far because she was getting older. When my ma died, my father was unable to shed a tear. He was not aware of losing his wife. He was no longer present. Before I left he told me he was afraid of not seeing me. The words had stayed in my memory.

"Elen..." I whispered. I raised my voice. "Elen... is my name!"

Red leapt into the air and landed right beside me. I crouched on the ground as if in pain. Red stood still, Brown and Wolfman too.

What will happen next? What if panic overcomes Forest Girl? These questions clamoured in the animals' heads.

I coughed. I placed my hands on my throat and coughed again. The coughing was getting louder.

Wolfman placed his right paw on my back and tapped me gently. Brown sat beside me.

"Forest Girl, we cannot take the flower away with us. We will come back as soon as we solve the rest of this puzzle. It only lasts one moon's period once picked. It cannot be preserved for any longer."

Red hopped on the ground before me. "There are guards set up to look after it from now on. The flower is one of its kinds and grows once a year. If we pick it we will ruin the chances of—"

"Noooooo..." I screamed.

The screech echoed in the still night, making Red jump.

I kneeled and pressed my hands on my laps. I screeched again, "He stole my heart!" Suddenly everything that had happened made sense. I now understood that the Forest Queen wanted me to presume that only a spell could make me see the Forest Queen and Red, as well as talk to Red and others. "It is safer that way," the Queen had explained to Red.

Brown jumped up, Wolfman backed away and Red pointed behind me. Brown and Wolfman crept towards the place Red had pointed at.

"Water Goblin stole the girl's heart in order to keep her forever."

The animals stood transfixed in disbelief, their mouths open.

"We need to come up with a plan. We might have to abandon the earlier plan for Red to befriend Mr Green's trustees. We need one plan for the girl to keep the discovery secret and another to get her heart back. But how? None of us can swim, except if... if he did." Red scratched his chin. He was on to something. They would get to the bottom of the pond and steal back her heart.

"Then we will ask the Forest Queen to fix the Forest Girl and travel back here to collect the flower, then send her back to where she came from." Having formulated a plan, Red's face lit up, and a warm smile lifted the corners of his mouth.

Wolfman pointed at me. "A discussion will take place later. The girl seems rather unsettled."

I opened my mouth and began to explain what had suddenly materialised in my mind. "My father has a disease that can only be cured by that flower's power. I walked all the way into this forest to find it otherwise the guards from the village will take him to the madhouse and my little friend Dash and I will be placed in a children's home that is like a prison, unclean and dark, with not much food... an orphanage!"

Wolfman interrupted. "That must be an awful place for a child to spend their time in." He turned his head away to hide the personal torture residing in him. Wolfman lifted his head and stared at the full moon residing in the sky, its light shining on us. At any time something unexpected could happen that would startle the little girl, Wolfman thought. He did not have much time. Emotions would only speed up the process. Pull yourself together, he ordered himself, this is not about you!

Red jumped on to Wolfman. "How long can you hold on for?"

"I don't know, my friend."

Red hugged his back and patted his fur. "It's not the right time. Hang in there." He jumped off, hopped on to my shoulder and back on to Wolfman's back. "Because your heart was stolen, your emotions can only last for a little while. Protect what you have, the memory of your father and your friend, but never show the slightest sign to Green that you broke his spell."

I stood up. "It certainly makes sense. Mr Green is the predator, not the wolf that attacked me."

Wolfman watched her. "You mean Wolfman?"

I lifted my arms towards my stomach, let them hold each other, then dropped them back down. "Certainly, sir. He persuaded me you were a bad creature wanting to kill me for food."

"Well, yum, yum…" Wolfman snapped.

Everyone began to laugh. I covered my mouth, Red jumped up and down on Wolfman's back, Brown wobbled. Nosy mice crept towards us, owls flew on to surrounding branches and joined in the laughter. Brown held out his right arm to the mice who rushed up it and nestled on his shoulder. "They are harmless," he said.

When the animals had quietened down Red insisted on going with me to ensure I returned to the palace safe, but Brown forced him to stay with him. Brown needed Red's assistance to protect the flower.

Wolfman approached me. "Well, Forest Girl, I promise not to eat you. We will be returning to the place we met Joy. He will transport you as far as the pond. Red has some issues to sort out tonight and a meeting to attend. Can you be brave? We will be waiting impatiently for you tomorrow night. You must be strong, never let Green know your memories have returned. Let's go."

I did not answer but looked around for Red. Brown turned towards me. Red was sitting in his palms.

"We will see you tomorrow, girl." Red nodded, displaying his little set of teeth. He lifted his arm, moved it from side to side. "Be safe, my friend, they will look after you. We shall meet you in the forest tomorrow."

The decision had been made by Brown who had not seen Red for many moons and was delighted to catch up on the story of their lovely girl.

10

The Powers of the Full Moon

Goblin walked into his palace and stopped a few steps away from an opening to the room where I slept. He extended his right arm and with the palm of his hand felt the curves of a new arch opening in the wall. He entered it. His eyes rested on badgers digging a vast space to accommodate his new weedy bed. He clapped his hands, smiled then whirled round.

Light came from the jars he had placed around the room earlier. He enjoyed catching fireflies. Outside, the crickets were becoming louder but apart from the noise and occasional frogs' whispering he felt the forest was extremely peaceful. The girl was safe, he insisted on telling himself, she would return. She had no choice; he was in possession of her heart. He shivered. I need to check on the heart, he reminded himself. It was in his top-secret cupboard.

"No, I cannot," he mumbled. He looked at the badgers working on his new bedroom and said, "It must be ready before the sun rises."

The badgers nodded. It had to be ready; these were Goblin's specific orders. Plans had been sketched out earlier by the master fish, Carp. Carp's abilities in drawing were spectacular, or at least that was what Goblin thought.

Having a bedroom each was a brilliant idea. In the winter he would not get cold as he wouldn't have to sleep outside any more. Well, when the summer was over he would set himself up in the new room. Green heard the sound of wolves howling in the far distance, and mumbled, "You will not spoil my plans! She is mine!"

*

Wolfman loped faster and faster while my grip tightened around his neck. The moon shone into his eyes, but he kept his head as low as he could. He shook his head, and I lost my right-hand grip. My reflexes brought it back towards his neck but he suddenly stopped, stood on his back feet and howled at the moon. I let go of his fur and fell to the ground with a thud, the left side of my body landing the ground first followed by my right arm hitting my upper body. The hypnotised animal could not restrain himself, it was too late, it was time.

Wolfman kept staring at the moon, howling and howling. All of a sudden I was blinded by a bright light. I pushed myself up to a sitting position. I rubbed my eyes and when I opened them I was able to make out a human figure standing where previously Wolfman had stood. I blinked a few times and my eyes were able to focus. A bare human, a young lad, stood staring at the moon. Hair covered his chest, beard grew on his chin and a moustache spread under his nose. Long, unwashed hair hung off his head and a large leaf tight with a rope around his waist covered his nudity. Facing the moon he opened his mouth.

"My apology for seeing me in this way. The moon's powerful rays revert the spells cast on me."

I stood to the left of the young lad. I extended my arm and touched his arm. "How is it possible you live in that animal?"

He took a step back, his arm slipping from my touch. He turned to me and his eyes met mine. "It is a long story and we are running out of time. It is not a long walk to the place where we met earlier. We will walk," he retorted.

My eyelids narrowed as I held his gaze. "We can talk while we walk."

Here was someone in exactly the same position as me, if not worse. I had to know if I had any chance of escaping, otherwise I would be Forest Girl forever. The wolf, now a man, grabbed me by my right arm just below my shoulder.

"We don't have time—"

"We do! Tell me what happened, how it happened. Who are you?" I was determined to get answers there and then.

We began to walk side by side.

"All I remember was growing up amongst wolves. They took me in as their own cub. To my recollection the mother wolf said I was left somewhere in the forests by a strange man. He never came back for me." He looked at me, his brows furrowed and his eyes narrow.

Pictures played in his mind of the moment, the moment described to him by his wolf mother. He did not remember it, he could not recollect it; he was too young when it all happened. His brows relaxed when I opened my mouth.

"You were an orphan. Your mother and father died, and the neighbours were forbidden from looking after you. Then one night your neighbour decided to save your life from growing up in the prison cells of the children's home. He brought you here not knowing if you would ever survive. The child that vanished, that story was told over and over again during my childhood. You would be beaten by the guards, work as a slave from an early age. He only wanted better for you. Maybe it was not the best choice—"

"No, he did what he did. It was fate," the lad said. His chest rose and fell as he breathed deeply. "The more I grew the less I looked like the wolves. Some tried to attack me because of the way I looked. In order to protect me we consulted the bad Water Goblin who cast a spell on me. Now the spell works as long as the moon is not in its full power, its shape. In this state I am as vulnerable as you are. Perhaps my body is still strong, but I would not be able to protect myself against a large predator."

I stopped. "Water Goblin knows that?"

The lad continued walking and pulled me by the hand. "He is aware that the spell breaks, its full power is affected. After I attacked him the other night, he will try to kill me."

I let his hand rest on my lower arm while throwing my arms into the air. "Great, so we are both in grave danger. He has us under his thumb."

"Not that fast, little girl." The lad turned to me. He grabbed hold of my arms above my wrists and looked into my blue eyes. His eyes narrowed and he blinked. "I have very little time before I am back in the wolf's body. I will protect you. I promise you will be with your father before the moon repeats three times."

My eyes left his gaze. "I don't have much time. The guards will take him away."

He wrapped his arms around my body. I leaned in and placed my head on his chest. I closed my eyes. The light came back, and the lad's arms released me. Long fur tickled my nose. I lifted my head. The wolf was no longer a lad.

"Goodness me, we are late, girl."

We giggled, I leapt on his back and we raced against the wind. We met up with Joy, said our quick goodbyes and went our separate ways, Wolfman took off in one direction, and Joy and I in the other. I thanked Joy for another ride in the sky, and this time I was brave. I watched the full moon as we landed not far from the pond.

*

The sun was beginning to rise. I was late. As I got closer to the pond, my eyes opened wider. Mr Green was standing on the banks of the pond talking to his frogs. If only he knew I had knowledge of his evil nature! The frogs lifted their heads towards me, and Goblin turned around to face me.

"Welcome, my dear. I hope you had plenty of adventures last night."

"Yes, I encountered some animals, owls and the like that are not afraid of the darkness of the night." It was a lie, of course. I couldn't tell the enemy about my new friends!

He pointed at the pond. "Glad to hear that. There have been some changes at the palace. You are welcome to explore."

"Thank you," I replied and dived into the palace.

It was time for me to find my heart, it belongs to me! My arms glided towards my body then away faster and faster. One, two, three, four, five... five moons had passed since I left Papa and

Dash and since the guard visited my house. I only have nine days left, if that.

The animals are devising a plan to find my heart. The one thing I can do is try to help in some way. The problem is I have no powers to open the secret cupboards. I took a deep breath and exhaled heavily. My eyes rested on my dress. The colour green as grass looked back at me. I had worn the dress for the past five days. I lived underwater, survived here without oxygen. My eyes moved towards my arms. They were clean. I shook then shivered. Oh no, Goblin will know. I have to sleep before he comes down. He must not find out. I raced into the dining room. There were two entrances. I headed for the new one on the right and peeked in. There was a bed made out of weed, like the one I slept on, same style, same length and the same width. How precise! I waved my hand at it then walked into the room I had been in for the past few days. I placed my hands on the wall of the bedroom, tapped around every bit of it, the bits I could reach, waiting for cupboards to appear unexpectedly. No luck. I slid my hands on the bedroom walls, no luck. He had put a spell on them! I dropped my arms, stumped my feet and walked towards the bed.

My body hit the bed lifelessly, my arms above my head. I should sleep on it. Tomorrow, or rather tonight, the animals might have a better solution. I will be seeing Wolfman tonight. He is a human like me. Two humans lost in an unknown world.

*

Red sat on a branch facing Brown after I left with Wolfman.

"Wolfman will enter his human state. With the power of the Forest Queen's spell he will search in the palace for the heart. It will be invisible to human eyes but with the Queen's spell he will be able to do almost anything."

Brown nodded. "Very good. I will guard the flower until you and the others arrive here."

Red spread out his arms. "If he finds the heart, and we are certain he will, he will bring it to the Forest Queen. From there everything is simple. Queen will transform the girl, but Joy cannot fly her to the village. That is Wolfman's responsibility. He is the only one humans would not fear so much, well, apart from me, but with my size I am not of much use to her."

Brown scratched his head. "The problem is who will distract Water Goblin while Wolfman searches for the heart?"

Red shrugged. "We will have to leave that to Forest Girl!"

Red and Brown hoped this operation would go smoothly. This was at least their fourth encounter with a human, and it had to stop happening. The more they exposed their world to humans the more they made themselves vulnerable. The girl, however, was a scarcity of nice humans. They couldn't punish her for what others might want to, or would, do.

"The spell was broken
The love was given
The humans are forgiven
The secrets must not be revealed!"

Red sang happily. Forest Girl had discovered her reason for coming to the forest. He danced, spun around and clapped his paws. The Forest Queen would be extremely pleased with him. He would gain another power. What should he ask for? He decided there was nothing he wanted; he was pleased with what he had. He might be promoted to a guardian of their world, to guard the spells, the many spells of the forest world. There was even the possibility of acquiring an invisibility spell that came as a free option with the guardianship.

"Yes, yes, yes!" he shouted as he hopped from tree to tree, branch to branch, occasionally breaking a weak branch. He was heading for home. Home was near the dreadful pond where the awful Water Goblin lived. What Red did not know was that Water Goblin was training an army for himself, an army against the unknown world, against anyone that crossed his path.

*

I opened my eyes, looked around and sat up on the bed. Noise was coming from the new room. I stood up and went to the entrance of the room. Goblin had placed some jars with fireflies around the walls, on a shelf rock strip. He had moved them to be in line with the flowers. One flower, one jar, in a straight line. This meant another set of fireflies would need to be caught every night. That would keep Mr Green occupied and out of the way.

I saw Goblin stretch out his right arm, and sparkles appeared at his fingertips when his thumb brushed them. A long drawer protracted in front of him. Oh, here we go! If I ask him what he is doing and how he is creating those drawers, he will not tell me let alone reveal the spells with their usage. This is impossible. The only time I had a proper conversation with that green creature was at the feast that has not been repeated since Wolfman's attack.

"I had not noticed you were awake, my dear. We shall dine in a little while. If you would like to get ready, I shall meet you above."

I took a step back, nodded and walked back to my room. How long did he know I was standing there? He had spoken politely, and he seemed a nice enough green creature, but it wasn't right to keep someone against their will, was it? No matter how nice he was, or how caring he might be. He only thinks of himself not about my needs, wants or desires. I was not meant to live in this place. I was not brought up in this damp green water, no, I was not.

Above the pond the sun was still shining, and for the first time I felt the warm rays as I walked out of the pond. I became aware of my dress and my hair being soaking wet. This was awful. I had not paid attention to this unnatural way of life for days.

We dined daily above the pond, and tonight we dined under the massive willow tree whose branches reached down to the pond. Green grass cushioned my feet like cotton slip-ons while I walked towards the willow. Servants, frogs mostly, brought us food on leaves. I sat on the grass, and in front of me stood a large flat stone which appeared to have been sought for the purpose of dining.

Food stared at us from the table before we sat down. The sun glinted in my eyes. I smiled, watching it set. Why was Water Goblin overly obsessed with not letting me out during the day? He must have a good reason. Most probably there were animals about during the day that could jeopardise his plan.

A hat gradually emerged from the pond, a face and then a body followed. Water Goblin looked up and a wide smile spread across his face, exposing brown uneven teeth. The frogs rushed around with food on leaves, and mice carried leaves on their heads filled with liquid. I inhaled the fresh air, the warmth that

I had been deprived of for many days. The smell of grass tickled my nostrils and I rubbed them. Oh bother, I must not let Water Goblin see. I have to ensure no strange, unusual words or sentences come out of my mouth. My arm slid beside my body. Be calm! He will not notice anything even though it is still daylight.

Goblin walked towards me, spreading out his arms and looking at the surroundings. "It is an early start for you today. The sun is still shining. My trust in you has increased over the last few days. You deserve to enjoy the pleasures of the day as well as the night. But only when I am around will you be allowed outside during the day. Only as far as the plain spreads, not too far from the pond."

A smirk appeared on Goblin's face. It was a decision that would make his guest like him more, a gesture of kindness. He knew that although she may or may not be fond of him right now, this gesture was certain to make an impact on her brain, the part he could not master wholly with his powers. He also did not wish to live with a zombie, he wanted affection. That would come gradually as the spell wore off and she would only have him around, he who looked after her daily.

I managed a smile. "I am grateful for your sudden decision. It is different out here when the sun is up." He must not know, I reminded myself. "I noticed a new room has been built. Was that the surprise?"

Goblin sat on the grass at the table opposite me. His legs created a circular shape, crossed at his sheens and knees apart. "Part of it. This is the other part. You may keep the old room or move to the new one. It is up to you."

I looked at the trees where the forest began. "Well, if I am occupying your room I have no problem moving to the new one, unless you do not mind me being there. You have so much stuff in the walls that it would take days to move, wouldn't it?"

Water Goblin lifted his head, his hat slipped backwards. He scrutinised my face.

"It will take a minute to solve that issue, oh, I mean, it will not take such a long time. Under the circumstances I believe it will be better if you stay where you are. I shall sort my properties tonight while you are exploring the world around."

There was no need for Goblin to feel suspicious as the girl knew he had stuff in the secret cupboards. But his crafty mind started playing tricks on him especially as he kept her heart in one of the secret places. She could not have known that but what if she was trying to find out this information? No, no, no, he said to himself. She has no knowledge of him stealing her heart! He continued staring at her face, the red cheeks that had never been red. Suddenly, his mind was racing. He clenched his fists, his eyes opened wider and his chest rose higher with every breath he took.

I felt some uncomfortable movements that Goblin was making and placed my hands on my forehead to shade the sun. "It is too bright. I am not used to this light."

Goblin's fists opened and his lips curled into a half-circle, exposing his teeth once again.

She did not break my spell, that was the sign. It is only her body's natural reaction to the sun, Water Goblin tried to reassure himself.

I placed a handful of blueberries in my mouth followed by some nuts as well as larvae. I had no choice but to hide my emotions by stuffing food into my mouth. My jaw moved up and down and my mouth closed as I stared at Water Goblin who licked the tips of his fingers. My nose swirled upwards. I can't do this. I placed one larva in my mouth and when Water Goblin wasn't looking, two in my pocket.

Two mice arrived at the table. Leaves filled with liquid sat on their backs. Four frogs wobbled on top of the table. They reached for the almost empty leaves we had just finished eating from. My fingers tapped on my lap. How do I keep the conversation going? It's essential the Water Goblin trusts me. If he does I will be able to enquire about his nature and hopefully the spells he is so indiscreetly using.

Water Goblin stood up and like a gentleman offered me his left arm. "Would you like to have a walk around the field, my dear? May I?"

My eyes widened as I placed my hand into his. "Oh, how honestly nice of you." There were larvae in my right pocket and disposing of them now would be very inconvenient. I swallowed hard. This will be very interesting. He let go of my hand and engaged his right arm on his hip leaving enough space for me to glide my arm in. I slid my arm through and gripped my fingers around his lower arm.

Water Goblin led me away from the pond and into the middle of the fields. He repositioned his hat then talked about the different kinds of flowers and what they could be used for, leaves that would make a brilliant green tea (if only teabags were invented). He pointed at the blue sky.

"I can lay in the grass and watch the blue sky all day. In the night when the moon comes out I ponder about its changing shape. It keeps me company during the long winter nights."

I raised my head towards the sky. "How interesting."

He stopped and brought me to sudden halt. "We are having a game night tonight. Would you be so kind to join me on this night?"

The kindness he was expressing towards me was surprising. However, I had a meeting in the forests shortly so I would have to decline the offer. But what should my excuse be? We moved on again. Silence resided between us.

I reached for my left hand with my right hand. "If I return early tonight I shall certainly join you, Mr Green."

Goblin's toes wriggled with every step he took. "Oh, certainly. Do not let me spoil your plans. Now will you excuse me?" He patted my left hand and I released my grip. I watched him dive into the pond.

I took the opportunity and squatted to dispose of the many larvae that were in my pocket. "There you go."

I felt the urge to run into the forest, but it was not yet time, it was not dark enough. What if Water Goblin or the frogs followed me? We could not afford to make any mistakes at this crucial time. I sat at the dining table, waiting, waiting and waiting. My face dropped into the palm of my hands. The sun began to form an orange tinge in the sky before disappearing altogether. While I sat waiting for the moon to appear in the sky I imagined my father talking to me, hugging me. He was walking, he was an ordinary human being and he was a normal person.

Light shone above me, I looked up. Fireflies flew above my head.

"Come on, come on," they whispered.

"Sky, blue sky, blue sky

Turn black, blue sky, goodbye

Black reveals new world

In which no one is bored

Now begins a new adventure!"

It is time for me to meet the gang, it is time to see them at work, see them debating, see them in action. Tonight the pieces will form a plan! I hope Water Goblin will not resurface at this time. I do not intend to join him at his game tonight. My nose lifted and my lips swirled as I took off into the forest.

The moon sat high in the sky, fireflies flew above my head and with every step I took they moved with me. This light might not be enough to see everything, but I had coped until now and I will cope again tonight.

11

Betrayal

The fish gathered around the rock table. The cards lay in the centre of the table and Water Goblin sat at one end. The green hat affixed on his head covered his face. His brows furrowed, his lips curled. He rubbed his chin. The girl had refused to enjoy a game with him. There was something out there that was drawing her attention away from him. Who was it? What was it? Who was conspiring against him?

He stood up abruptly, his hands placed firmly on the table. Would the wolf be involved? The wolf that came to ask him for help! Ha, ha, ha. He would not be able to fight the master of arts, the one that had created him! He smirked at the realisation, his arms loosened and his body slammed back on to the hard rock he sat on.

What about the Forest Queen? She had more powers than him, she was the keeper of the mountains and the forest but not the rivers or lakes. She had followers all over the forest-populated area. The Queen was a kind Queen, but she was angry at him!

For the hundreds and hundreds of years of his life that he had spent alone in this forest, in the pond surely he deserved a companion. The humans changed from decade to decade. Before, they never used to enter the forests; now they were entering the forests more often, disturbing the lives of animals, killing some, eating some, capturing the weak. They would not dare to come as deep into the forest where he lived – he would destroy them in a second. Justifying his actions made him smile. He was powerful, no one would ever beat him, he assured himself.

The fish had laid out the leaves on the table. It was time to play, to relax. He lifted his right arm and a fish swam to face him.

"Send a team to spy on the girl, ten frogs precisely. Now!"

The fish left.

"Ha, ha, ha, ha!" Water Goblin was content.

*

Wolfman walked into my path and I took a step back.

"Forest Girl!"

The corners of my mouth rose, my eyes widened. The wolf is a human being like me. He understands my predicament. I walked towards him.

"Hello." I leapt on to his back and grabbed hold of the fur around his neck.

It was time to reach a conclusion about how to recapture my heart. They were all in effect blindfolded as they lacked the ability to search Water Goblin's mansion.

"The meeting is taking place only a few yards from here," Wolfman said.

The birch trees we passed appeared to be talking to each other. Their branches reached out to me and some touched my hair and back.

"Have you noticed that? Do they do that to you?"

Wolfman turned his head sideways. "Yes, they are curious about others. You are a human so they must be even more curious about you."

The team was seated facing the tall, fat ancient oak tree that stood casually in front of them. Wolfman stopped and I climbed down. Red waved his arm at me.

"Forest Girl, finally."

Joy, Red, Brown, Wolfman and I all sat on an overturned log, probably caused by lightning many, many moons ago. Forces of nature, Forest Queen called it. She had no powers over the sky. Peace spread in the forest. Red stood up.

"Here we gather to ask you for a solution to our slight crisis. It is Water Goblin that we are up against, whose powers are great and frightening."

The Forest Queen opened her branch arms as if to hug us all. "How can I help, my friend?"

Red's eyes never left her gaze. "We have learned about the Water Goblin's improper keeping of the girl's heart. In this way he has an advantage over us all. There may only be one way to discover where the heart is and remove it from his possession."

"Which way would that be, my dear?"

Light shone on our heads from the fireflies flying in a circle above us, and I lifted my head to greet them. The Queen lifted her left arm, a branch with three forest fingers, towards them.

"Shhh..." she whispered.

The animals noticed but paid no attention; the fireflies were always around.

Red sat on the wolf's back. "Wolfman can swim if he is in his human state. If we equip him with another power or two, he would be able to see through walls, see things that we cannot see. Then if he could breathe under the water, which means become a reptile for some time, let's say one day, he would be able to search for the heart."

"We can equip Wolfman with all the powers you have just mentioned. This task will not be easy and of course someone will have to distract the Green monster for Wolfman to enter his mansion," the tree said.

I spoke up. "I shall persuade Water Goblin to hold another feast. The pond will be unattended as the fish will be under the influence of the magic drink that he offers all attendees. The frogs will not notice either as they will be busy serving food. This will work."

I wanted it to work but had not realised I would have to entertain Water Goblin so that he would not notice Wolfman entering the pond.

Everyone was so delighted to hear the girl's voice that they missed what she had just said.

Wolfman cleared his throat. "We will have, or better said I will only have, very little time to accomplish this mission. If everything goes according to plan—"

Leaves rustled and branches cracked behind us. Then all of a sudden, frogs hopped on to the animals. The green creatures wore helmets and body armour and held shields. They had been following Wolfman's trail.

The Queen morphed into an ordinary tree while the animals had to defend themselves against spears laced with poison. The attack started and because these green animals were so tiny they had an advantage over the large predators. Once the spears pierced their skin, if not treated, the poison would enter their bloodstream and kill them instantly.

Wolfman had two frogs on his back. I was standing next to him and grabbed a branch from the ground. I knocked both frogs away, just in time as one of them was holding its spear in both hands ready to stab Wolfman in the back.

"Deadly target," I exclaimed.

The blow smashed them against a tree trunk, and a green sludge streaked from them. The tree gave out a peculiar "ahhhh" – it certainly was not happy about the green blood on its trunk!

"Thank you," Wolfman managed to mumble then continued to fight with the rest of the animals. He stepped on one of the frogs by accident then lifted his paw and pulled a face at the green stuff hanging off his paw. "This is nasty! What does he feed them?"

I laughed, although the rest of the team were lucky to kill the many attacking frogs without getting stabbed themselves.

"Not one of them got away!" Brown said.

Red was very unsettled as he hopped about on the trees. He started to gather other squirrels. These ones had no powers, they did not belong to the special team, but they were his friends.

He started to organise a look-out team. "This will do for the moment. We need to act quickly. These animals followed you on orders from Water Goblin and as they will not return tonight Water Goblin will be asking if you had seen them," Red explained.

"I shall deny it," I said, confused.

"Yes, you did not see them!" Red repeated.

This latest development had put their plans at risk.

"You must return at once. We will search for any other soldiers that may have overheard our conversation, but I believe there are no more. Hurry back. Tomorrow night he must prepare the feast. We will take care of everything else. Be very, very careful. This creature is suspicious of your actions," Red warned.

I felt completely bewildered. The very calm meeting had ended up being a war zone. Wolfman licked my face as I sat subdued on the overturned log that was now sprayed with green blood.

"You be careful, girl," he said.

She could sense his kindness and understanding from the words he spoke and the expression on his face. He would be here forever while she had a chance to escape! She lifted her head to face his large furry head. Their eyes found one other, her blue, his deep brown.

"I will save you!" he said quietly.

Then Red hurried her to go, alone, but he sent many squirrels to guide her.

It started to rain. The moon was covered by many clouds and the forest was dark, but she was not far from the pond.

*

I entered the palace wide-eyed and out of breath.

Water Goblin was sitting at the table playing cards. It was his favourite game. I felt a twinge of guilt but knew I had to hide it as he might be able to read it in my expression. He looked up, his hat still on his head exactly as he always wore it. The only time his hat fell off his head was when Wolfman had sent him flying in the air. His wispy green hair was exposed then completely. He was going bald.

"An early return? Has anything happened?" Water Goblin enquired innocently. He knew none of his army would return to the pond. There were forces against him out there and even if the girl was not involved with his enemies, his army would be killed because they were his followers. They were ordered to strike at anyone that was talking to her, anyone, innocent or not!

"It started to rain. The forest is like an unlit castle." I used the forces of nature as an excuse, but I knew they were present tonight in order to protect me. I smiled at Water Goblin. I had a plan. "May I join you?"

"Of course," he said, delighted that whatever had happened out there had brought her to him. He had everything under control, he had her in the palm of his hand.

The fish were glad she was joining them as it meant the game would be fair now. They all had fun and laughed at Mr Green's serious face when he lost. Then he laughed with them at himself. They had fun when she was around.

I made a suggestion. "We should play this game at the feast, well, that is, if we could have one." I dropped my eyes to the floor.

Water Goblin had to make her happy. He wanted her to remember his kindness when the spell he'd put on her memory wore off. He fixed his eyes on me and scrutinised me before announcing, "We will have a ball tomorrow night."

He would protect the pond and its surrounding area by tall walls, trees, holly bushes, stinging nettles, anything that would distract predators and the wolf.

Once the game was over, everyone scattered in different directions; the fish to their respective places of living, and Goblin decided to work on his special wall.

*

"Water Goblin is suspicious now. She had done something for him to send soldiers to follow her," Red said to the animals.

He was unhappy that the Forest Queen had to witness a horrifying fight that had killed ten frogs. None of them had escaped their fate. They were all under a spell when they attacked; it was not in their nature to take on or attack other animals and cause them harm. But as the rain washed away the green blood once again they arrived to ask for the Queen's help.

She expressed her disgust at the blood that had been shed before her. Red and the others apologised as sincerely as they could.

"It was inevitable," she added, making them feel just a tiny bit better. The Queen equipped Wolfman with X-ray vision, the ability to breathe underwater, and just in case he had any unexpected encounters she also gave him the power of invisibility. "These powers will only last for three moon changes. Be careful how you use them," she warned. Before she disappeared she said, "Do not enter the village in order to find out what happened to your parents. It was fate. Come back with the girl and her heart."

Wolfman could not help thinking she knew something he did not. She refused to change him to the wolf he was now but accepted his actions. But he could not question her motives. The Queen was a very wise tree, with more powers than he could ever dream of. And he had been knighted by her many, many moons ago when he dissuaded the human race from entering the forests from this particular side.

Being a knight was nothing though; he still had no special powers other than being massive in size and strong in nature. Was it because he was a human inside that she would not give him a power?

"It is not because of that," Red said, trying to console Wolfman. He'd read his mind, an unfair move on his part.

"Thoughts should be kept secret. They are private. What if I thought how beautiful that Forest Girl was, would you mind, my friend?"

"It could have crossed your mind. It's only a human nature, isn't it?" Red responded, adding, "Brown thinks she is a stunning being."

"Wow, wow, wow... that is something you should have never, ever... No, I had no such thoughts!" Brown cried.

They all laughed, momentarily released from the prospect of the dangerous task that lay ahead.

*

I felt both excited and nervous about the next move. I had put myself in a dangerous position, but somehow I trusted Wolfman. There was no set plan about how this evening should unfold. All I had to do was make sure a feast took place tonight. The feast was the distraction, a cover for Wolfman.

I began to feel anxious and paced from one bedroom to another, waiting for Water Goblin to enter the palace. This had to be the day. What if Mr Green did not allow me to enter the forests tonight after the celebration? He had a good reason not to trust me any more. His army would not return from spying on me. But was this really what was worrying me so much? Would he keep me captive? If he finds out my real intentions, the whole plan could fail. Stop! Stop! Stop! I said to myself, still pacing between the two rooms. Water Goblin must see me smiling, happy, unchanged, the way I was previously.

Fish swam into the palace. Excitedly, they headed towards me. There were about fifteen small fish, and behind them six large carps were holding a piece of garment in their fins. As they came closer, I gasped at the new, sparkly blue dress they were delivering.

"It's beautiful!" I said, as it was gently placed on my bed. When I turned to admire it more carps entered the room, this time bringing a long bow that was meant for my hair. It was quite the fashion these days, but how did Water Goblin know about fashion or about the village? Never mind, the foxes must have told him!

I reckoned Water Goblin had created them using magic. The items looked upper class, royal family style clothing. It seemed he wished to host a pertinent ball. The servants exited, leaving me to dress.

I sat on the weedy bed. Next to me was the ball gown I would be wearing to impress Mr Green, whom I would betray, who had stolen my heart and kept me captive against my will.

I slipped into the blue sparkling dress that reached below my knees. It was tight at my chest and hugged my flat stomach. The sleeves were puffed up at the shoulders, making the dress look more formal. I felt comfortable in the dress. Now I had to sort out my hair. It was wet though, and unless it was dry the hairstyle would not look appealing. This was the way Goblin lived and he did not mind the wetness of clothing, let alone his hair. There was no mirror in the palace, nowhere I could see myself.

The fish began to reappear. They were equipped with hair-brushes, and others were carrying my new blue sandals, and smart gloves that were of the same material as the dress. The fish untied my hair, treating it with respect, and brushed it gently. Then they tied the ribbon around my head, and it spread through my hair. My new shoes were ready to be worn. Some of the fish impatiently forced my old sandals off and placed the new pair on my feet.

The fish swam around in amazement; I looked stunning. Water Goblin will be pleasantly surprised. It was time to get me above the pond.

12

The Mission

Mr Green rushed around the grass plain. He set apart a larger space, planted four elm trees in a square then ordered fireflies to create decorative lightning. The fireflies laughed and continued flying around.

"I am prepared to use magic unless you do what I ask," he threatened.

They flew in a half-circle between each tree. Rock tables were again set up in three long rows, small rocks beside them served as chairs and leaves with golden painted names were placed again correspondingly.

Mr Green looked at the plain, his eyes resting on a lit square where they all would dance tonight. He spun round, paced to the pond and squatted at the water. "It's time. Deliver my presents. Hush."

Mr Green stood up and straightened. A smile formed on his face as he passed the frogs busy preparing the evening tables. He stopped under the willow tree, his body shaded by its long branches. Uttering some magic words, his usual clothing changed into a tuxedo, green of course. His hat was green with a red ribbon hanging off it. He reckoned if everything went well tonight the girl would even fall in love with him. But right now he just wanted to make an impression. He knew he could not cheat his own spells.

The corners of his mouth rose as he stepped into the presence of his great green servants and spread his arms out towards them. "Atara tata," he said.

All the frogs' attire changed into tuxedos, green with shirts and bows. They wore hats that were very similar to their master's, the only difference was the red ribbon. These frogs were clumsy, they would certainly stumble on each other's ribbons and cause an incident that Goblin could do without.

"Wow..." The frogs admired one another.

Fireflies formed a large circle above the three rows of tables. The full moon emitted bright light. The shape of the moon was expected to remain the same for another few nights, Water Goblin was sure of it. He studied the moon's changes thoroughly. It delighted him that the moon was the wolf's downfall, him being a human in disguise. If it were not for his spell he would not be the large predator that every animal feared. Well, he cannot pollute his mind with thoughts about the wolf, he decided. The party will start now, he must choose some songs to sing, and an opening speech as well.

*

I swam above the pond with the fish around me, enjoying the sparkling shine my dress gave out. Some of the carps ahead of me emerged above the water and chanted, "The girl is ready and coming out now."

The Water Goblin stood at the spot where I was about to emerge, already holding out his right hand as low as he could. I came up with the ribbon still in my hair. My eyes were fixed on Goblin as I accepted his hand. It was a gentlemanly gesture that I was not to resist, no matter what kind of man he was.

His eyes scrutinised me. I was wearing the garments he'd sent me. His eyes widened with surprise at how perfectly the dress fitted, how my long brown hair made a difference when it hung loose. Not only did he watch my figure, he seemed mesmerised by my blue eyes.

This was a moment Water Goblin could frame. He would store that special memory of beauty.

"You look... handsome," I forced myself to say. The only other thing I could have said was that he looked "different", but I feared he might be offended, and we didn't have time for that.

He escorted me to a special seat: the middle table host chair. Everyone could see me, admire me, and everyone had a chance to view my beauty.

A leaf with my name as "The Girl" was taken away instantly by a frog servant before I had even sat down. My eyes kept scanning the area around me, the frogs and what they were doing. Since my feelings had returned I was aware that anything could trigger a strange reaction, so I needed to stay focused. The less feelings I showed the more chances I had of pulling this off.

Water Goblin leaned towards me. "By the way, the dress looks delightful on you."

I faced him. His green eyes were glued on mine. "Thank you. Thank you."

"Pleasure." He stood up then walked away to give a speech now that everyone was seated.

He stood before the head of the table. "Welcome everyone!"

"This is the day we celebrate.
We drink, we feast, commemorate
Dance together, don't separate
Become friends, move, dominate
Humans, animals, lovers or none."

As Mr Green brought his speech to an end I raised my arms and vigorously clapped my hands. All the animals joined in. It was overwhelming for Mr Green to be treated in such an extraordinary way, accepted by many. It was an extreme pleasure for him, these animals loved him! And the girl did too, or at least that was what he desired. He picked up a flower top with some liquid in it and toasted tonight's event.

"To our pretty princess!" It was a toast, not an obligation, for me to become their princess.

All eyes were on me. I raised the flower glass and drank the mixture.

Many frogs gathered at a spot that acted as a stage: three fallen logs. They started the evening by croaking in very different tunes.

Goblin walked over to me, and offering his right hand invited me to dance. The potion I had just drunk was making me feel very happy, uncontrollably happy.

The pair attracted many other pairs on to the new dance floor that Water Goblin had designed. The animals were showing off their dance moves, standing on one paw, spinning around, chasing tails. Goblin grinned at me. "Marvellous, isn't it?"

"Yes, Mr Green." I had to force the words out of my mouth.

*

Red sat on a branch not far from the pond watching Brown in tall grass monitoring "the party at the pond".

"It is not as complicated as you think." Brown, a large furry animal but sensitive in nature, faced Red. "I will linger around the forests in front of the pond and keep an eye on the festivities. If anything or anyone acts distrustfully I will report to you and you can warn Wolfman."

Red's eyes glinted. "Correct. I will endanger my life in order to let him know that something is not right. I will create waves in the pond using my tail. The waves will hopefully reach him before Water Goblin does." He threw his arms out as Wolfman walked into their conversation.

"I am ready."

A circular white ball sat in the sky and shone at the Goblin's party which began with frogs croaking crazily. This was "the time" they had all agreed. Wolfman howled at the moon for a while then a young man appeared in front of Red and Brown. He circled his arms about and shook his legs.

"Joy is missing tonight?"

Their eyes widened at the young man in front of them and Red hopped on to Brown's right shoulder.

"Haven't seen you in this way for many years. You have grown up, son."

The lad looked at his hairy chest then nodded. The corners of his mouth rose. "That is the fur that I can't shake off completely."

He is something else, Red thought.

The lad imagined being invisible and he disappeared suddenly.

Red wiggled on Brown's shoulder then chased his tail and giggled. "Ok, ok... this game is unfair."

The lad reappeared then waved goodbye to Red and Brown as he caught sight of Joy approaching the team.

Everyone, including Joy, chanted, "Be safe."

Joy turned to the group. "Isn't he a handsome man?"

They nodded then went about their tasks. Joy was the standby transport; he and Red had discussed an action plan in the event of an emergency.

*

The lad cautiously emerged from the forest, stepping carefully to avoid making any noise. In front of him was a wall made of bushes of alpine currant and holly trees. New elm trees stood around the pond. He rolled his eyes and shrugged his shoulders.

"This Green creature is a very clever Goblin."

He climbed the holly tree wall that prickled him as he jumped over to the other side. The sound of frogs croaking was getting louder. He avoided the festival side that spread out to his right as he approached the pond. On his left he encountered the very old willow tree. As he walked, he observed the participants of Green's party.

Green's frogs were all smartly dressed, matching Green's outfit. Then the lad spotted the Forest Girl. She was smiling at the Green creature, dancing with him, holding his froggy hands. Yuck, the lad thought, as he pulled a face. He could not take his eyes off the girl. She wore a sparkling dress that hugged her figure and her hair looked different when it hung loose. She was the princess of that ball.

He pictured himself dancing with her but then the girl was overshadowed by Green, which jolted the lad from his dream. What was that? He shook his head. He had never experienced such a feeling before; this was something new to him. Carefully placing his feet in the pond to avoid creating waves, he slowly submerged his body. He tried to glance in the girl's direction one last time, but tall reed mace grass stood in his way.

Every animal knew that Green's palace was situated at the bottom of the pond. The lad was here a long time ago. Nothing seemed to have changed. He pushed the large stone and created waves that would most definitely attract the fish, but he quickly put the stone back to ensure they would not notice it. Although no one could see him, it was imperative for him to be extra cautious. One wrong move and Green could discover him. The lad imagined his special vision and his vision changed. The walls became transparent, and he could see drawers, cupboards and wardrobes. There were many clothes, strange items, leaves, a golden pen, jars, lids, glass tubes... What did the Goblin not have? The lad swallowed hard and shook his head. He progressed from one room to the other.

His attention was drawn to a bedroom with the girl's clothes on the floor, her sandals too. She must have left in a hurry. He picked up her blue dress and pressed it to his face. It was impossible to smell the dress underwater so he let go of it. He scanned the bedroom and again noticed the large amount of clothes. Did this Water Goblin really enjoy wearing all these clothes? He had only ever seen him in green clothes, green hat, same every day, every week. But he must change regularly considering the many shirts, trousers and even funny green sandals. The garments were exactly the same, identical in fact.

The lad turned around and faced the weedy bed. His eyes widened as he looked directly above the bed. His heart pounded heavily. There it was, a solitary jar on a single shelf sitting above the girl's head as she slept, keeping her company. After all, the beating heart in the jar belonged to her. The lad turned around a few times, scanning the room. There was a problem: he lacked the special abilities required to remove the heart without a trace and without destroying the soiled walls. He sighed in frustration. There would not be another feast to distract the Goblin. It had to be today, now.

He entered the last room that was unfamiliar to him and scratched his head. He would have to access the heart from this room. Make a large enough opening in order to remove it.

And so he did. He soiled the opening, smoothed it and prepared to leave. He held the jar in his hands, covering it fully with his palms, and it became invisible. As he watched the jar with the red heart vanish in his palms he spotted a carp emerging from the first bedroom into the small passageway that connected the other bedroom. He froze, forgetting he was invisible. The carp swam right past him, very close to his hands that held the jar. It headed for some secret drawer and pulled out a green handkerchief. The fish had knowledge of magic otherwise it would not be able to access any secret drawers. The Water Goblin gave the least harmful animals powers, like the frogs they killed! It must not see him. Although there was very little chance that the carp would be able to see the lad, he was still very anxious. A permanent frown resided on the carp's face as if the task of collecting something for the master bothered him. It left the room without noticing the lad.

He shrugged his shoulders and relieved some tension in his muscles. It was time to leave. He left the new room in the same state he had found it. Although he had replaced all the soil, he could never be certain he did not leave any traces. His body would be changing back to a wolf soon, and wolves cannot dive. As his head emerged above the water, he spotted Red on the willow tree. Could Red see him if he was invisible? There was no way he could, he thought.

The lad walked slowly towards the tree. When he was just a few steps away from its trunk he turned around to see what was happening at the ball. There was a lot of noise coming from the other side of the pond. His eyes scanned the dance area and found the girl who was still dancing with the Green creature. She was smiling and spinning around happily, seemingly without a care in the world.

What did the Green beast do to her? He clutched the jar tighter while his blood boiled within him.

"It will break," he heard a voice say.

Red was standing beside his right leg. He waved at Red to move then they both walked away from the palace.

Red only knew he was there because he had read his mind, he could hear his thoughts.

Naughty little creature, the lad thought as they entered the forest.

Red chuckled. "I heard that!"

The lad shook his head. "I told you it is not very fair to do such a thing."

As they walked further into the forests a light appeared from nowhere. Red stopped for the now transformed Wolfman. Their eyes met. Who had the jar? Then Red noticed it on the ground at the roots of a tree. It was there, it was safe.

Wolfman ran towards it, picked it up and inspected it. "It's fine. Not the slightest damage to it."

With his tiny paws pressed on his hips Red noted, "That's lucky!"

Wolfman did not reply but handed it to him. The jar was as tall as Red himself.

"So, am I to look after it?" Red asked.

"Yes, jump on me and hold on to it."

The jar was just a bit too big for Red's paws, and he could not place it under his shoulders either. He sat on Wolfman's back, placed the jar on the wolf's spine and covered it with his body. He could only just reach the wolf's fur with his front paws. This was very dangerous, but Wolfman would be careful, Red thought. They were only playing with someone's heart!

They entered the Forest Queen's residence and were unexpectedly greeted by her.

"Good work, my friends," she said as Red presented the jar to her. The branch hands enveloped the jar. Three branch fingers on each side of the jar let go and the jar sat on the Queen's palms.

"Blessed be." The Queen observed the beating heart before placing it into her trunk. The trunk swallowed it instantly. "It will be safe with me. Bring the girl to me swiftly."

The tree stood still again, no moving branch arms, no eyes and no mouth. There were no other instructions, so all that remained was for Wolfman and Red to join Brown and Joy watching the ball.

Wolfman sat up between Joy and Brown which made Red slide off his back.

"What is it?"

Wolfman did not answer but Red moved his tail from side to side. Red jumped on to Joy so that he could be at Wolfman's eye level. "What is it, Wolfman?"

"Water Goblin might not let the girl out tonight. It is dangerous for her to stay in, especially after interfering with the palace wall." He was becoming paranoid as he stood up next to Brown observing the frogs dance their strange dances, listening to croaking sounds. If Red read his thoughts one more time he would get very angry! Very angry!

Red jumped on Wolfman's back and whispered, "She will be fine."

"That's not what I was thinking," Wolfman retorted.

"She is under his spell now. The smile is induced by a spell," Red continued.

"She looks beautiful when she smiles," Brown said, joining in.

Wolfman could not bear to watch any longer. He turned around and sat abruptly, facing the many trees around him. Red hopped off his back just in time and joined Brown at his left shoulder.

"Princess," Red said loudly enough for Wolfman to hear.

"Yes, she might be Water Goblin's princess soon!" the wolf retorted, still motionless.

Red turned around to face Wolfman, his paw on his hips, his tail tapping the ground. "Water Goblin has no rights on her. Would you let him?" Red spun back round and continued watching the ball.

There was no reply from Wolfman. His head hung low. What was happening to him? He needed some fresh air. This place was suffocating him, especially as Red could read his thoughts.

When Red turned around again, he couldn't see Wolfman anywhere.

"He left," Brown said.

"Typical. He can't face an argument or discussion."

Wolfman did not go very far. He found a large tree and sat on the damp soil behind it. "I hope you do not have special powers," he said to the tree.

There was no answer. Wolfman's head dropped once more. He used his right front paws to scratch the soil in front of him, in slow motions, up and down. The girl could never like him, the furry animal he was, the ugly paws and nasty face. Why would she? Although he was a human in a way, he had no parents, he had no record of who he was. Who could ever trust him? The villagers most probably knew each other, their lives, each other's personalities, deeds that they were known by.

And he was no one, fatherless and motherless, a child left to the wilderness when only a baby. The girl will choose someone from the villagers, a man with a history, not an animal like him, let alone a Goblin.

Joy approached Wolfman. "The party has ended. Only the frogs are left, cleaning up the mess."

Wolfman stood up on all fours, staring at Joy. "Where is the girl?"

"She seemed happy as she left hand in hand with the Goblin into the pond. I don't think she will be returning..." Joy said warily.

Wolfman shook his head. "You think... you can't. She doesn't like him. There is no possible way she would... or would she?"

"I believe it is a cover-up, but knowing the Green creature she could just as easily be under the influence of his spells."

"Which means?"

"Which means she might give her consent to marry him. If it's a written consent, she will have to marry him even when the spell wears off! It is the law!"

"Law? What law? Who defined this law? That's an illegal enforcement!" Exasperated, Wolfman left.

He had to enter the palace and find out what was going on. This waiting was killing him. But he could not, he was no longer a human. He could use the invisibility power but Water Goblin would spot him, most definitely. He could not get close, Green's wrath could kill him.

13

Transformation

I spun in Goblin's arms as he grinned into my face, but I was not disgusted by him. Why? It was the drink, the drink influenced my emotions. As long as Wolfman fetches my heart and keeps it safe, I could distract Mr Green, which seemed to be working perfectly so far. The fun was nearly over, though. Green as usual gave a speech but he spent most of the night dancing with me and drinking that spell liquid. He forced me to drink many flower tops filled with the fluid. I laughed as Goblin wobbled a bit. It was time to end the festivities.

"Dear friendsss and othersss
Be safe in the wildernesssss
We will meet soooooon again
Another ball, the main!"

The frogs clapped eagerly when their master suggested a main celebration, a wedding perhaps. I had no idea what the words meant, I only hoped Water Goblin would let me go now although it would seem impolite to disappear after the celebration. He led me into the pond, my hand in his arm like a married couple. He was establishing the bond.

My eyes flew to the bushes where light glistened. Was that the team watching me? And was Wolfman amongst them? At the thought of Wolfman I tried to pull my arm free of Goblin's grip then stopped. It was not a good idea. I laughed for no obvious reason as I looked at his green face.

In the palace Goblin carried me in his arms from the door until he reached my bedroom, where my clothes lay on the floor. As he lowered me down this was the moment Water Goblin had been waiting for: he was to kiss me goodnight. His big eyes stared at me, his head moved a little closer to mine. Oh no! I swung on to the weedy bed. It was the best move I had made that night, and now he had lost the opportunity to kiss me!

He was not annoyed by this. He could not force me otherwise I would refuse him too early. He picked up my clothes from the floor and held them in his hands. Seeing me lying on the bed, he bade me goodnight as he made to leave the room with the items still in his hand.

Without turning round, I replied, "Goodnight."

He smiled at that, it was an achievement for him. He assumed I liked him, but in my mind it was more "goodbye".

*

Goblin lay above the pond, his eyes focused on the stars. Frogs jumped about picking flower tops and leaves from the tables and the ground. He clicked his fingers and changed their appearance back to no clothing. Fireflies still kept the green frogs company, their dedication for tonight would be rewarded. Maybe he would use them as an army of insects equipped with deadly weapons. He never considered fireflies being on the Forest Queen's side. Wolf was not around this time, somehow. He had missed all the excitement. Will he visit next time? Goblin wondered.

"Master, there were no bodies found but we think we saw some blood splattered in one particular area. The wise tree residence," a frog reported, breaking Goblin's train of thought.

His green face lit up and the corner of his mouth curled into a smirk. "You suppose the 'Queen' would..." the smile widened further "would have killed them as they passed by?" Then his voice rose. "She is too kind-natured to have done something like that!" He sat up suddenly. "Something unusual is happening, and the fat tree has its fingers in it!" His fist clenched, and if anyone could see inside him they would see his blood boiling with rage. He murmured to himself, "She cannot destroy my plans." He raised his finger at the frog as he instructed, "Tomorrow you and your team of many soldiers, not just ten, will follow the girl. You do not attack unless you are attacked. Do you understand? Then you report to me on her whereabouts. I do not trust anyone, Gummy!"

Why did he call his best frog Gummy? He named his servants anything he wanted to, they were his, he owned them! His plan was to train the army to use weapons effectively. The grin returned to his face when the frogs jumped off into the distance and he lay back on the grass. Watching the moon, he revisited the events of the ball. He'd had a fantastic time, and so had the girl.

"Ha, ha, ha, ha... she will be mine!"

*

I slept through the day and when I finally woke up, Goblin was bringing a new series of fireflies for the palace. He seemed to be in a good mood, and I wondered what might have caused this. He had only managed to catch enough fireflies for the front room and my bedroom; he was unable to carry any more jars. I stood up from the bed.

"Are there many more to catch? Do you need my help?"

"It will not be necessary." He turned to face me once he'd placed a jar on the shelf. "Dinner was served already. I have left..."

I fiddled with my fingers. "I don't feel hungry."

Feel? She cannot feel! Had the spell worn off already? That is impossible, Goblin thought.

Observing his face, I noticed his eyes had narrowed as he scrutinised me.

"I think," I added.

The Goblin stopped staring at me, his eyes fell to my skinny dress.

Do not worry, he reassured himself. This is not the time yet; the girl is only being a human.

I placed my hands on my sides. I must fix this. "My apology for being difficult."

"That is fine with me."

Now will he let me go? I am in a hurry. How am I going to make him feel comfortable letting me go? "Thank you for the dance at the ball yesterday."

"You are welcome."

I continued to talk while I watched him walking about with the jars. "I had a wonderful time."

"I did too." He faced me. "Are you leaving for the forest now?"

My face lit up and a smile formed on my lips. "If I may. There is so much to see."

And because he could not stop me as I would only resent him for it, he waved me out in a "you are free to go" gesture.

The clothes I wore were too nice to ruin, but I could not care less right now, I was about to leave this Green creature forever.

I ran out of the tall reed mace grass that surrounded the pond. My dress restricted me a little so I held it above my knees to move more easily. As I ran into the forest I kept turning back to look at the pond just in case Mr Green wanted to stop me. He could have discovered the heart was missing.

As I reached the forest I began to relax. He had no powers beyond the pond, the Queen had said. Only his trustees could attack me now.

*

Water Goblin was in the new bedroom collecting all the jars. The fireflies in here were dying, and he was beginning to feel sorry for them. He let them out, caught new ones and returned the jars to their respective places. Fussy Green creature! Remembering he had nothing to do tonight except remove his stuff from the girl's room to his new one, he got to work. The important thing was to create a secret drawer; he had only managed to make one for his handkerchiefs earlier on.

Standing in the new bedroom he faced the wall that was furthest from the entrance. As a vision of the drawers formed in his mind he clicked his fingers. In that instance many drawers appeared in front of him, all empty, ready to be filled with clothes. They were long in length, one drawer could hold clothes for at least one individual. Why did he need so many? He just loved the extra space.

A frog walked in, uninvited. "The army is ready, Master. First bunch of fifty soldiers are already following the girl. The other fifty are ready to be led by me, sir. On your command." Its arms were at its side as it stood to attention like a human.

Goblin's face lit up. "It will not be necessary at this moment, Gummy. The girl will return, she has no choice." Mr Green laughed. The drawers disappeared in the wall, empty for now. He had many more to create.

The frog scratched his head with his left hand. "Shall I put them on standby?"

Mr Green did not reply. He was visualising his new wardrobe facing another wall. He clicked his fingers and there it stood. Large, spacious, it could hold many shirts and coats, tuxedos too.

"Yes, Gummy. Let them practise battle moves. I want them ready at all times!" he answered finally.

He thought the wardrobe was perfect. It closed and vanished in the wall. He faced the side of the wall that connected to the girl's bedroom.

"At your command, sir!" the frog answered, marching away.

"Just in time," the Goblin muttered.

In that part of the wall was the girl's heart. He could take a closer look at it. He devised his plan for the drawers then clicked his fingers. Drawers appeared again in front of him, and there was a wide space on the wall where no drawers were fitted. With his green frog-shaped hands he started to push in each drawer until the wall was as it was before. He took one of the jars from a shelf and faced it closer to the spot where the heart was.

The Goblin was moving his head sideways, looking very closely at the spot on the wall, his nose nearly touching the soil.

Then he placed his right hand in a print. It was a print of a human hand. A clear print of a human hand, it was nearly as large as his which meant it did not belong to the girl! Someone else had been in his palace while he was out, while he was... He punched the wall where the print was, creating an imprint of his fist. He clicked his fingers and opened the spot where the heart was meant to reside. It was empty. The heart had been stolen!

"Agggggggggggggrrrrrrrrrrr!" He screwed up his face, clenched his fists and stormed out of the room.

Above the pond he met Gummy.

"The team must undertake a mission right away. Prepare all soldiers and contact the vicious foxes!" the Goblin ordered, furious. The battle had started now! "The wolf," he muttered to himself, walking around in a circle. "The wolf!" he repeated. Who else could have had the human form to imprint a hand on his wall? He was fuming. This wolf did not realise he had actually left a print of his palm!

Had he been foolish to host a ball for the girl? Was he being set up by her and the wolf? Does the Queen have her fingers in all the pies? His frogs had most definitely been murdered in front of her. She must have witnessed the killings, and allowed it! Surely, her nature would not have allowed it. But she had witnessed it, which was enough against herself, against her throne! Having the power to intercept the killings, she chose to ignore them. For a human! Bad choice, bad choice. Goblin was considering all the options to overrule the Queen. He would bring her down, but first he must kill the wolf!

"Move forward!" he commanded, wobbling slowly with them.

*

Red faced the members of the team.

"The girl is in the forest, heading for the Queen's residence. She has frogs on her tail, they are closing in on her. I do not believe she is aware of it. They will not attack her, only follow her."

Wolfman interrupted. "The Queen will not perform any transformation if there is disruption around her residence. We must ensure a clear path for the girl. We must attack!"

Red pointed at the deer. "Joy, you meet up with the girl. Keep her safe. You, Wolfman and me, we fight the frogs!"

Brown lifted his arms. "How about me?"

Red patted him on his right shoulder. "You keep an eye out for another wave of frog soldiers."

"Great idea."

The friends spread out in different directions. Wolfman and Red ran alongside each other.

Red caught his breath. "I knew this would happen."

"I did not expect otherwise."

Red turned to Wolfman. "More blood will be shed."

Wolfman smirked. "Only the frogs' blood."

Red fumed. "They are animals as much as you are!" He realised Wolfman was a different sort, a human-animal kind.

"Maybe," Wolfman added. "But they are under the influence of bad spells. Unfortunately, they chose their fate as well as their master." As he finished his sentence they encountered a large number of frog soldiers.

Wolfman stood still, waiting for the frogs to attack him. Red did the same.

All of a sudden, spears began to fly towards the two animals. Red hopped on to the trees then jumped out to attack the frogs. One by one he killed them instantly; he was far too fast for the many soldiers equipped with spears and deadly poison.

The frogs ran holding their spears above their heads, ready to attack. The wolf swung his right paw as they approached and sent a large number of frogs flying into the air. He watched them hit the trees, his head jerking as one by one they smashed against the trunks. His eyes closed for a second.

"Ouch!"

Red pulled a face. "That was not fun to watch."

"Hmmmm, I am having fun." He swung his other paw and sent more frogs flying into the air. The frogs were not very strong opponents so it was a boring battle for Wolfman. He breathed in and bellowed, "Come on!"

A spear swooshed in the air, landing just in front of his front left paw, almost touching his long claws. The poison on the tip of the spear would have paralysed him, if not killed him. Nothing can kill me, he said to himself confidently, although he did not fully believe this.

The frog that threw the spear had only a shield in his hands now. It watched the wolf move forwards. Then the frog turned and ran, but it would never outrun Wolfman. The wolf stepped on it with his right paw.

"Oh, there you go, that is for being a coward. Yuck." He lifted his paw, but the green blood stuck to it like glue.

Seven frogs cornered the swift squirrel against one of the many trees. Red kept backing away until he touched the tree trunk, his eyes wide, his paws in front of his chest.

Their spears pointing at the animal, the frogs croaked, "Now we've got you!"

Red whistled to Wolfman, pointed at the frogs and gestured with his right paw a straight line across his neck. The frogs turned around, and on seeing Wolfman they panicked and started to run in different directions.

Wolfman charged towards the group and as soon as he reached them they flew three by three into the air. His mouth exposed his sharp teeth in a broad smile. "This is fun."

Red's knees gave away and he wobbled trying to regain his balance. "I do not think so! I do not need to remind you we are actually acting against nature! And by the way, I am ok."

Wolfman looked at him. "Sorry, my friend, I was chasing after one that was brave enough to throw a spear at my front paws."

"Thank you."

Wolfman patted Red on the back. "You are welcome, my friend."

Red nodded. "I am all right, all right."

They continued the fight until there was not a single frog soldier standing.

Red raised his arms in the air. "We will miss the transformation of the Forest Girl!"

They rushed off to try to reach the Forest Queen's residence on time.

*

I arrived at the place where some moons ago I was attacked by Goblin's army, the place I first discovered a talking tree, the Forest Queen. Here I will be transformed back to a human, an ordinary being.

I spotted Joy. It was Joy who flew me above the many trees to meet Wolfman. Then I met a bear who found my treasure, the flower I had come here to look for, some many moons ago. Now, I am about to leave the forest creatures behind, the friends I have made, and I will probably never see them again. Well, until next year probably when the treatment wears off. Next year I will avoid the pond!

Joy bowed his head. "Good evening, my dear. The Queen is ready, but the others are not here just yet. You have followers, soldiers on your tail," Joy explained, his deep voice ever so calm.

I faced Joy and managed to give him a peck on his left cheek. "Thank you. Thank you so very much."

Joy blushed, his head moved to the other side. "Hmmm."

The Queen opened her eyes and extended her branch hands. There was the jar containing my heart. "Finally you are here. I have kept this for you since last night."

My face lit up and a smile formed on my lips. "He did it!"

Wolfman appeared from behind a tree. "Who?"

I gripped my hands together tightly. "You. You did it."

"Oh, yes. Did you doubt me?"

"No, never," I said.

The Queen took out the heart, and using a spell that cushioned the heart blew it towards me. It floated on a light cloud then as it reached me it stopped for just a moment before travelling through my chest and into its natural place.

I gazed at the Queen, my body still with fear. Then I felt a warm glow all over my body. My cheeks became redder, my hands regained warmth. Blood started to circulate in my veins. The Queen clicked her branch fingers and the spell changed my lungs to human lungs again. I felt my toes tickle as blood flowed into them.

"Oh, thank you so much. Thank you, my Queen. I don't know how to thank you enough." I dropped to the soil, kneeled and kissed the tree roots.

"You are welcome, my child. You must keep this world secret otherwise humans will destroy us. Promise me."

"I promise."

The Queen cast a spell on my promise while I kneeled at her roots.

Red began to wave his paws against that but felt a large paw on his tiny mouth as he attempted to speak.

"You must not interfere. It's for our own protection," Wolfman whispered. "Seems you got too close to the girl, that you forgot where you come from," Wolfman added.

Red pushed away Wolfman's paw. "No. I haven't," he said quietly.

I rose from the floor and turned to the animals, all except Brown, and thanked them. I approached Red and hugged him tightly. "Thank you so much, my friend. I shall never forget you."

Red started to sob but did not say a word. Then Wolfman ordered the girl to let go of him and jump on to Joy's back.

"We will meet at the mountain," Wolfman said.

The Queen waved. "Until next time, my dear. This is not the last time."

As Joy flew off, Wolfman faced the Queen. "Not the last time? She will come back?" His eyes widened as he scrutinised the tree.

The Queen simply closed her eyes, her mouth disappeared and her branches stood still.

"Questions should be answered, my Queen!" Wolfman said angrily and left. Not the last time? What does she know that she is keeping to herself? Wolfman disappeared into the distance as Red continued sobbing on the branch next to Forest Queen, and Brown approached them, out of breath.

"There are many more coming this way. Amongst them are the wicked foxes. The Green creature had just equipped them with powers—" Brown stopped, turned around and around until he spotted Red sitting on a branch, lonely, sobbing.

"She is on her way to the mountain," Red said, between sobs.

Branches cracked nearby. Two foxes appeared and attacked Brown with spears. The bear was large and extremely powerful, but the foxes were crafty and overpowered him. They had also overheard where the girl was heading to – the mountains, but which mountains? The two foxes had spotted Red on a branch earlier but he was no longer there.

"The squirrel will lead us to her. Come on!" one shouted to the other.

"Well, move then!" The other pushed his mate forward, ignoring the large bear who was lying unconscious in the Queen's roots.

As soon as the foxes left the Queen enveloped Brown and sent healing powers through her roots to try to save her honest follower, the gentle giant. She succeeded in saving the bear for now.

"You can't take what is mine!" Her anger at Green threatened to boil over, but she was a wise tree and knew not to interfere with anyone's fate. This was not Brown's fate, but only she knew this.

*

Joy landed between two mountains far, far away from the pond and the village. Wolfman arrived breathlessly as Joy was engrossed in conversation with the girl.

"We have no time for chit-chat," Wolfman said with a smirk.

"Well, finally," they chanted.

"Ok, ok. I have no wings to fly with, unlike you, sir," he said, defending himself.

I watched them challenging each other and wondered if they were joking or really arguing.

"My dear, we only tease each other. This is our way—" Joy attempted to explain but Wolfman interrupted.

"Hop on."

I impatiently sat on the wolf. I wasn't far away from home and my papa. Holding on to the fur of the large animal, I even forgot about the brave action this wolf had put up the previous night. I forgot this animal was a human in disguise, a human who had been left in the wilderness many years ago.

I thought how proud my papa would be but also how angry he might be when he found out about my adventure. In his own way he must sense my absence, he must know somehow that I am not around the house, but he cannot ask, he cannot reveal his concern.

*

Wolfman trembled as they passed the many pine trees and headed for the plain on the steep mountain top. It was that time again and he just could not control it any longer. Why now? he thought. This girl is in danger, Water Goblin must be following them and the frogs are playing with poison. Why can this stage not pass so that I can bring the girl safely to the village and never see her again? That was a horrendous thought. Had she captured his heart? he wondered.

Then the wolf became a man, in a blinding light that engulfed a large area of the forest and might possibly have been seen by their enemies.

*

The lad turned around to look for me. I was on the floor, knocked down by the sudden transformation. He offered me his hand and pulled me to my feet.

"Are you ok?

"Yes, thank you."

He gripped my left hand and pulled me up abruptly, only to tell me we had to continue up the hill on foot.

"Sorry," he muttered.

"It's not your fault," I said.

"Are you prepared to go back to the village?" the lad said, trying to keep the conversation going.

"I have lived in the village all my life. It is my home. My father will be pleased. He will be able to walk, talk and be free of the strange illness."

"What do they call you in the village?" he asked, realising that no one had registered her name when she had cried out on seeing the flower for the first time.

"Elen. My name is Elen."

"Nice name."

I felt him watching me and tried to change the subject. "Is there a way to undo the spell that changes you into the wolf?"

"I do not believe so. Only Water Goblin can undo what he has done. Do you think he will remove the spell after...?" He suddenly became anxious, unwilling to talk about his situation. "It's not important," he added.

"You are a human..." I began.

"For now. For a while!" he uttered. He let go of my hand.

His head hung low, shoulders hunched. "Do not bring my humanity up again, please."

I took hold of his hand again and locked my fingers in his as he watched me. He stared at my pink face. My blue eyes met with his.

He pulled my hand. "Let's go."

They reached the spot where the flower stood, glowing in the dark night.

"It's time to pick it," he said.

Red appeared from nowhere on one of the trees and offered me a glass jar. "This is for you, my dear. Place it inside to keep it safe."

As I leaned in to pick the flower, I observed it for a moment.

"I have an army following me," Red added, trying to hurry me along. "Two foxes killed Brown."

I gasped, nearly dropping the jar. "No!"

The lad hugged me as I mourned Brown's unconfirmed death. Tears rolled down my cheeks for the first time, they felt warm and wet. The lad's kind gesture made me feel protected and cared about, then light came in and Wolfman stood before me, watching my disappointed face.

The girl could never love a wolf! And I am a wolf! A wolf-man! She has a life in the village, he has a life in the forest. He is an alien to the villagers, the village and their way of life. What an excuse, he thought, he is an excuse, a living excuse!

"Contradiction, isn't it?" Red said.

"Not again!" Wolfman faced him angrily.

"Maybe you'd like to know—"

"No!"

"She…" Red began, then stopped.

"Interesting," Wolfman said. "Isn't that a private issue?" he added.

I wasn't listening to them. I was admiring the flower and grieving Brown's death.

"Brown is in her mind right now," Red whispered quietly.

Wolfman turned towards him. "Of course." Wolfman turned to me. "We need to get you to the village."

I jumped on to Wolfman's back and offered my right arm to the squirrel. "Red, are you coming, my friend?"

Red shook his head. "No, my dear. You will be safe alone. I will try to discourage the soldiers."

Tears forming in my eyes, I waved. "Please be careful. Will I see you soon, my friend? Will I see you ever again?"

"Entering the forest again might kill you. The Goblin's anger might cost many lives. Whenever you are lonely look beyond the first trees of the forest. I shall be watching you." He hopped off a branch and on to another, jumping further and further away from us.

I started to feel different, as if I was about to lose the experience I had had with these extraordinary animals. They belonged in the forest, and the only way to encounter them again would be to return here. Now I am forbidden by Red to enter the forests. The friends I created, I saw on nightly basis, I talked to, I laughed with were about to vanish from my life. But why?

Wolfman said, "Sometimes it's wise to listen and obey the ones that are experienced."

"But I only have Papa in the house, and a little brother that I just housed who had no one else. Whom will I talk to?"

"Your father? The boy?"

I giggled. "They are not as chatty as Red is."

The path from the top of the mountain was long, treacherous and steep. Wolfman was vigilant, stopping at any unknown sound. I held on to his fur tightly and pressed my body on to the animal's back to camouflage myself.

My dress was rather bright for such actions, but I was unaware of the attention it might attract.

14

Home

The Goblin lifted his arms high in despair.

"How has this happened? The girl is most probably on her way to the village. I want the army to split into two. One follows Gummy, the other follow the foxes. Do not keep me waiting too long!" he had screamed earlier at the frogs. He only had fifty frogs on the move, and now they had split in half, that was only twenty-five in each direction.

He managed to walk to the Queen's residence where just a while ago his army had killed the large bear. They had poisoned him. Good job, little ones, the Goblin thought. But the bear was not there now. Where was he? Had the Queen disposed of him? He laughed straight at the large tree. If he came face to face to fight that large trunk of hers he would win the battle!

A voice echoed in the distance, "Very confident, Mr Green."

Red was hiding in the forests, on a tree branch, sitting not far from where Water Goblin stood.

Someone was taunting him, was it the Queen? Was she playing tricks on him? Water Goblin turned away from the tree and then back. She was starting to make him nervous even though the tree had not moved a single branch.

But then it felt like the surrounding birch trees were closing in on him. That can't be possible, he thought. Their branches were reaching out to him, some hitting his face and shoulders, others hitting his knees, as he started to walk away from the Queen's residence.

He sped up and bellowed, "These trees are annoying!"

There was no one around to fight with him. He had no powers, nor did he have any strength in the forests. Still, he was overly confident he could win a battle against the Queen. He raced away but could not avoid the punishment for daring to challenge the Queen. The trees hit him in slow motion. They took turns, as if they were enjoying each hit.

The Goblin arrived back at the pond and happily gasped for air. What an experience, he thought. One of the foxes ran into him, causing Goblin to lose his balance.

"Watch out!"

The fox did not apologise as he said, "We found a trail going to the mountains. Gummy is following it."

Goblin rubbed his hands and smirked. "That is very good news, very good news." His eyes narrowed. "Where is your team?"

"They are headed for the village. Most likely the girl is on her way there."

So his army had separated just as he ordered them. It would be rather pointless for the whole army to go to the mountains after overhearing part of the big bear's conversation with the Forest Queen. Goblin knew they needed him to give them orders and directions.

Now he just hoped they would do the easy bit: beat the wolf and bring the girl back to him.

*

The foxes were extremely crafty, similar in nature to Mr Green. Corruption was in their blood.

One of the foxes returned from reporting to Mr Green, out of breath. "We are heading for the village," it confirmed.

Their team was slow. These frogs were useless, anyone could beat them!

"We will go ahead of you, little frogs!" the foxes uttered slyly.

There was no way they would wait for that jumping lot. As the two foxes progressed on their own, they sheepishly exchanged looks, their mouths opened in wide smiles.

"Army of idiots!" They laughed.

Before them was a steep slope that they had to climb downwards. This was the part the foxes hated when returning from the village. Goblin had equipped them with spears, just as he had done with the frogs, but the foxes had disposed of them as soon as Water Goblin was out of sight. They did not need those useless weapons of his! They had done fine using their own paws and teeth until now, so why should they change tactics? If they could bring down a large bear why would they not be able to bring down an oversized wolf?

They were unaware that Water Goblin had cast more spells on them. He would not be beaten by a wolf. They rolled crazily off the steep slope and ended up bashing their bodies on the rocks at the bottom.

"Ouch, ouch, ouch...!"

Their bodies were still curled in balls as they landed.

"It's ever so painful rolling down that tall slope! But always fun," they said, laughing as they uncurled.

"Can I take you to the dance floor, dear?" one said to the other, offering its paw.

"Oh dear, you may." The other laughed sheepishly.

They danced and danced, spun each other around like humans do. They mimicked Goblin and his guest dancing the other night.

"Ha, ha, ha. The wolf stole Goblin's prey. Wolf will marry a human. Ha, ha, ha!"

The foxes knew Wolfman was partly human, and they also knew he could never return to being a human. Would Goblin allow him to be a human again? As they danced they could hear and feel some movement not far from the slope.

"They are here." The foxes hid in the bushes close to the bottom of the slope.

A rock fell down the slope, hitting other rocks on the way.

"Stop pushing!" The foxes began to argue.

"Get off my paw."

One of them stepped hard on the other's paw in revenge.

"Don't you start now, sleazy fox!"

"Wait! They are going down the slope."

They peaked through the bushes but seeing some spears land at the bottom of the slope, they decided to wait for the pair to move further forward.

*

I got off Wolfman's back.

"This place is dangerous."

We arrived at the slope I had climbed many days ago. As I looked below a stone flew down the slope.

Wolfman tugged my arm. "Let's not make too much noise. We will attract the soldiers."

I kept quiet. Up to now our journey had been very straight-forward, almost too good to be true. Was Goblin lurking some-where around here, or was he waiting at the bottom of this hill?

"Attack!" they heard someone cry from below. Frogs with poisoned spears!

Wolfman pointed at me. "Elen, get behind me."

I took a deep breath and bellowed, "They are not after me. They will not hurt me. It's you they want to kill."

The frog soldiers formed a half-circle in order to close in on their victims. They held their spears above their heads. There were many, so many that I lost count, and many more were still arriving.

From behind Wolfman I asked, "What shall we do?"

He whispered, "Jump on me. We are going down."

I jumped on and grabbed his long fur just in time. He turned at the slope without hesitation and jumped on to the rocks. He used his front paws as breaks as well as his bum. It was a rough ride for Wolfman especially as he was carrying a passenger on his back that could be injured by a spear at any time. He tried to bal-ance his body but at times he felt I might just roll with him.

We landed at the bottom on countless rocks and I lost my grip and was about to land face down on the rocks. But just in time the wolf felt there was something happening and caught my dress in his mouth. I hung off his mouth horizontally, face down, staring at the rocks below me as I clutched the jar with the flower in my hands. I froze.

"Don't drop me!" I said.

He used his front paws to verge me gently on to the ground. I smiled.

"Thank you."

He lowered his head. "It's my pleasure."

Somehow, he was no longer happy in that wolf's skin; he did not like me to see his face and body deformed and furry.

Two foxes jumped out of the bushes next to us. They landed on Wolfman, ignoring me completely. Sharp nails dug into his fur and skin, and he bellowed in pain. He swung his right arm as one of the foxes bit deeply into his skin. The fur did not protect him as he began to bleed from the bite, but he did not care about the pain any more.

The foxes attacked him relentlessly. As soon as he pushed one off his back or leg it jumped straight back at him. He defended himself effectively, but each attack left him with a wound. The foxes were under spells, two, to be precise. One for speed and one for immediate recovery. They were unable to die from any impact; the only exception was if they drowned. That was the downfall in Mr Green's plan; he could dive so he expected everyone to be able to do the same.

With my fingers gripping the jar, I stood nearby observing the fight. My eyes rolled at the sight of so much blood so I took a long thick branch of quite fresh substance and slammed it at the foxes like a cricket bat. Each time they tried to jump on to Wolfman I swung the wooden bat at them. I was fully aware of what

I was doing there: I was helping my friend who had helped me so much already. All I could do was return the favour.

Wolfman opened his snout, exposing his huge, sharp teeth as he glared at me. "Go, Elen, run to the village. You must leave now."

I stood still. "No. No, I am not leaving you here with those vicious foxes."

They screamed as they prepared another attack, "Vicious?" They approached the wolf daringly, but I stood in their way.

They will not attack me, they want me alive, they need me alive. Then I snatched the glass jar, hopped on to the wolf and kicked him in the ribs to spur him on. In pain, he leapt up seconds before the foxes jumped at him, and we disappeared into the forest.

Trees hurtled past; Wolfman's speed was incredible considering the kick I'd given him. Wolfman was no match for the foxes. Once I was safely in the village they would not be able to do anything. They cannot force me to go back to Goblin.

After a while in the air Wolfman mumbled, "That hurt, girl!" adding, "You damaged my ribs."

I defended my action with a smirk. "That was the only way to escape."

He tutted. "Right."

*

We arrived close to the garden my parents owned. The fence was high, impenetrable, and a gate was visible from one side. This was it. We had only a split second to say our goodbyes.

"Will these wounds heal? When you change to a human will they still be there? Permanent scars?" I asked, touching the wounds on his left arm after one of the foxes brutally bit him.

Wolfman observed me. "It will heal. I always have the Queen to help. You must be careful."

Tears began to form. "I am home, Wolfman. You are the one who might need help facing those foxes!" I brushed my hand over my right cheek and on to my hair. "Will I see you again?"

Wolfman used the back of his paw to wipe my tears away. "I don't know. The forest is dangerous for humans. Do not come back!"

I held his paw. "So long and again, my friend." I let go of his paw and walked towards the gate.

"So long," he said, very quietly. He placed his paw on the ground and watched her walk away as he whispered to himself, "And soon, my friend, soon!"

He lowered his head as he watched her safely enter the dark house. Seeing a window illuminated he was ready to walk off. Then he heard squeals of joy from a child, Elen's friend, the boy she had talked about, a parentless boy like himself.

He remembered the foxes were still after him and they would want to kill him now that the girl was safely home. He had to find a way to kill them, although he did not relish the thought. He hated killing the necessary part of nature and reproduction. Still staring at the light in the window, he left slowly, heading to the Queen's residence. There was something he wanted to ask her; actually he needed two pieces of advice.

*

My fingers enveloped the rusty handle of the front door as I pushed it down gently. It opened and I walked in. A warm feeling filled my heart. I was about to see my father and Dash, but then an image of my new friends who I would likely never see again sprang into my mind. I reached for a candle that I could just make out in the darkness, and the matches next to it. Illuminating the kitchen with the candle I saw Dash approaching.

He screamed, "Finally!" as he ran towards me. "You came back."

He hugged me as I squatted down to his height. Our faces touched and we both sobbed happily.

"Where is Papa?" I whispered.

"He is asleep."

But as he said that a large figure emerged in the doorway to the kitchen leading to the bedrooms. The person was only just able to walk, a fragile old frame of many bones but no flesh.

The man in the doorway was supporting his body by one hand on the doorframe, and he was trembling. He wore a nightgown that consisted of a piece of old rug pulled through the neck. It was off-white, most probably unwashed for the many days I had not been there.

Although the kitchen seemed clean in the little light, only tomorrow would tell how much dust had settled in my absence. Dash was only a boy, he could not have known how to tidy up and dust the place. I placed the jar, which I was still clutching, on the table. It was safe there for now. I walked towards my papa.

His eyes were fixed on the jar. "The flower!"

"Forest that kills

My daughter knows

Lost for many days
What happened, she never says."

As my papa finished his speech, his grip on the doorframe loosened and he began to fall to the floor, but I caught him just in time. With Dash's help I walked him back to his bedroom. I hugged and hugged him. There were no tears on my father's face, but I knew he was pleased I had come back.

In the morning I will let him have the tea and then he might warn me or tell me off for being so gullible to enter the forest. I had promised to say nothing about the lost world, the different word, and I must keep my promise. Soon the horrible guard would return but my father will send him away! Never to return, because next year I would be eighteen and old enough to look after myself and Dash, my new little friend, my half-brother. I peeked out through the kitchen window and observed the garden where I had parted with Wolfman.

When I did not see him or his shining eyes I went to get some rest in my bedroom on my soft bed for the first time in a long time.

*

Wolfman was not far from the village when the foxes crossed his path, their tongues hanging out.

"What a surprise!" They smirked and glanced slyly at each other. "If the master can't have the girl, he will be pleased with your head instead."

"I am sure he would love that, but you'll have to catch me first."

The foxes leapt into the air, but Wolfman stood on his hind legs and with his front large paws he hit them in the chest, sending them flying far into the distance. By the time they recovered the wolf had vanished.

One of them shook his head. "What was that?"

The other fox scratched his head. "Anger!" He jumped on to all fours. "Anger has made the wolf rather powerful."

Foolishly, the other fox asked, "Who angered him? You?"

The fox pushed him away roughly. "Definitely not me!"

"The green creature will destroy us. We had better hide or follow the wolf."

Just as he said that the frogs cornered them. Gummy was in the lead and pointed his spear at them. "Take those two with us."

One spear in their leg and they would be dead, at least that was what they thought. They did not know Water Goblin could cast recovery spells, so they did as the frog said.

*

Wolfman entered the sacred residence of the much-loved Queen. Her arms opened, awaiting him, but he was not one for cuddles so she let her arms drop.

"Nice to see you, my friend."

"Queen, the girl has been delivered. How is Brown?"

"He survived the ordeal. We had a little chat then he left for the mountains. You should visit him soon."

The wolf smiled in relief. "How about Red? Is he around?"

The tree blinked a few times. "He is, he is. You have some questions for me, my friend?"

"Yes, my Queen. Two foxes are on my tail, unbeatable, under some spells. Is there a way? I mean..."

The Queen would not kill a creature, but she could advise him how to defend himself. That way it would not be a deliberate killing! Her eyes closed and her eyebrows furrowed.

"I shall express my deep, deep sorrow at this matter, but you may consider water as a means. Though this is not the only question you desired to ask."

Lowering his head to the ground, he spoke. "I have been wondering for these past few days since I met the human girl that I was a human also, I have that human in me. Would you ever be able to change me to human again or am I lost forever?"

"You are not lost forever, but I cannot reverse what the Green creature created. You must confront him or stay a wolf forever. Once the girl does not see you, she will forget about you."

The Queen knew this was not the case, but at this stage it was the only solution; the wolf had to live in the forest now. The wolf kept his head down. He didn't have time to worry himself thinking about whether the girl felt what he felt. What he felt? Did he feel anything?

The Queen changed the subject to the issue of the foxes. "I have no doubt that you will fight rightfully."

He lifted his head, looked into her eyes then bowed before she could disappear. "Oh, my Queen, I promise."

She watched as he turned to leave, saw his pain and reached out her branched arms behind him. Her fingers only just touched his furry tail, but he did not turn around to say goodbye. He didn't need to this time.

*

"You failed me! You failed me! I trusted you! You disgraceful dirty lot!" Water Goblin was greener than usual, spreading his froggy hands and pointing his froggy fingers at the foxes. He continued to shout as the foxes bowed their heads. "You had powers to use, you were indestructible animals! How did you fail to kill that disgraceful animal?"

They turned to each other. "We had powers?"

One answered the other, "Probably. I thought I didn't feel anything when the wolf hit me."

Next to the pond the frogs formed a circle around the foxes and Mr Green. Their spears were pointed at the foxes until Water Goblin gestured for them to lower their weapons.

He screamed desperately, "You will look for the wolf. And do not return until you have his head in your paws!"

The girl was not coming back to him, he was to live on his own again! What had gone wrong? he asked himself.

"I am guessing the girl is safe at the village?" he spat.

The foxes nodded. "She, she... she is, my master."

The Green creature threw his head back and shouted into the cold night air, like a wolf. His "No!" must have been heard in space.

The foxes left freely, knowing the wolf was to be killed now, sooner rather than later. The frogs let them walk away but pointed their spears at them again. The Goblin would not be happy until the wolf was dead.

As he walked away he ordered the frogs to follow the foxes' every move.

*

I greeted my father excitedly. "Morning, Papa."

He sat in his chair at the kitchen table. My father did not speak, only observed the yellow flower. I boiled some water and placed the bright yellow flower into it. Its colour flowed and dyed the surrounding liquid yellow, then blue and green. The tea was special, a rainbow tea. Not all the colours of the rainbow but a beautiful mixture.

I offered the tea to my papa. I pressed a metal teacup to his lips and as he opened his mouth I slowly poured the mix into his mouth. I patted him on the back. "Well done, Papa."

Dash watched the transformation unfold. The man that had only spoken an occasional riddle, if at all, the man that could rarely move and mostly stared into space was about to become a different human. Was it possible?

I washed off the yellow colour from the cup. "Papa?"

My father replied, "Yes, my dear child."

I left everything I was doing and hugged my father. Dash was speechless, staring at the man that had never spoken to him before.

"Thank you, my dear daughter."

He stood up to greet Dash, but the child could only look at him in disbelief.

I broke the silence. "This is Dash, Father."

My father hugged the little man and thanked him for looking after him. "The days that we waited for Elen to return are over." He added, "My son."

Dash now belonged to a family, he was a son to my father, and a brother to me. This was such a joyous day.

I sat at the table once my father had settled back in his seat. His skin started to look healthier immediately, and his cheeks looked pink. My father was now a healthy man again. Although he was ageing and no longer young, he started to look better.

My father began, "My darling daughter, the trip you decided to endure was the most dangerous thing you could have done. But I must thank you for your bravery. You do take after your mother, who never gave up on me. She knew where the medicine grew. But each year the flower would choose a different spot to grow on."

I stared at my dad and held his hand that had wrinkled with age. Dash held my left hand in support.

"One day next year I will revert to the same fragile man I was just a minute ago. Then I do not wish you to ever return to the forest that holds so many secrets no human should ever know about." He said no more, but I had to know what he meant by that.

"What secrets, Father? What happened that you do not wish to share with us?"

"If I have to, then I will, my daughter, only if I can deter you from ever going back to the forest."

He wanted me to promise I would never enter the forest again, but I could not do that. There was no way I could let him become the frail, weak man again next year.

"Continue, Father. I would like to hear—"

"Your mother knew what happened to me. She died with the secret in her heart," he said.

I lowered my head at the thought of my ma, my ever so hard-working mother, who never once complained.

"One day in the village news spread late at night that our neighbours down the road here, the farmers, had passed away from some illness. Both the wife and the husband. Villagers believed the excessively cold weather had killed them. In the couple's old age they had a son. The mother gave birth to a long-awaited son not many weeks before they died. But the son took all her strength and she was becoming very ill. The father looked after the boy and his wife day and night, but that night he died clutching his wife's hand and holding on to the crib where his child slept."

I listened patiently to a story I partly knew already, with Dash still holding my hand. He came and sat on my lap as my father continued with the story.

"I ran into my neighbours' house and seeing the child still asleep, I took it into my care. But my wife explained it was impossible to keep the newborn child and that he would be taken by the ministry and placed into a kids' dungeon. If it survived one more day then it was lucky. She cried. I took matters into my own hands and walked into the forest. The boy was wrapped in big blankets in a small crib. I left him that night under this large tree that looked so peaceful, so safe. I planned to return in the morning to feed the boy, and I would do that every day until he grew up. But suddenly the tree opened its eyes, grabbed the child into its strange branch arms and placed it into its trunk."

My father covered his face with his palms and tears rolled down his cheeks at the memory of what he had done. The pain of it had stayed with him ever since.

Dash was intrigued. "That is impossible," he said, but my father ignored him.

"The tree then said that I was guilty of giving a human being to the wilderness and she could never forgive me. She did not give me a chance to explain and condemned me. She said that because I had seen her, I had seen this different world, and for that also I would have to suffer. So she protected the world, herself, by casting a spell on me so that I would never ever tell anyone what I am telling you now. But one day she told my wife about the cure, about the flower but I had to keep it a secret forever. If I failed to do this, she would not create the flower every year for me. And as I am telling you this, the flower will not grow next year. I broke my promise. I do not know what happened to the boy. I pleaded with her to look after him. Now twenty years on the boy should have been back two years ago but he did not come back."

My mouth fell open, my eyes grew large and my tongue stayed still, heavy like a log. I listened to the story of Wolfman, the wolf that helped me, saved my life. I was familiar with the story, now I understood it was my father who had abandoned him in the wilderness. He was our neighbours' son. Their house still stands there after twenty years. It has never been occupied after they died. Nobody wanted to live there. A child had been stolen from there, there was something abnormal about it, everyone was saying.

My father sounded upset. "The tree has the answer to the secret, to my peace of mind. The child must be somewhere."

I could not say that I knew the child was a wolf now, I could not say what had happened in the forests. No story involving magic will come out of my mouth.

There was a knock at the door. It could be the guard returning as he promised he would.

When the guard saw my father at the front door all healthy and talking his face became pale. "I mistook the house. I was supposed to go to—"

"No, soldier, you are not mistaken but next time you see my daughter, speak to her with the highest respect because I shall be after you. And here, my new son Dash wants to greet you."

Dash walked out next to my father and held him around the waist.

"Sir, my mistake!" The guard bowed and walked away.

My father was a farmer like many in the village. He sold his crops of wheat and was a respected man. Next year his daughter would be eighteen, a grown-up. She would be able to face the guard herself if he decided to barge into their home again.

*

The foxes were on a hunt, they were like sniffer dogs following fresh trails. One led them to the Queen's residence which frightened them. They turned away instantly and without waiting for her to appear, rushed away.

Wolfman was in the den, occupy his spare time with the many cubs around him.

"Come on!" he shouted.

He wanted some time off now, but they persistently walked all over him. And as he walked outside the same cubs stood still on his back, some holding on to his fur, others holding on to his legs.

"I need a break," he muttered.

One by one they got off and left the sad wolf alone.

"You ok, my dear?" Sef asked, but he just passed by without answering or even looking at her.

He was off into the forests, to his special place. As he lay there he thought of the Forest Girl, Elen, her pretty face, her kindness, her humanity that he did not have except once in a while. This pretty human was in his mind all the time, he wanted to see her, know her better, but he could not. He could not sleep. It was getting darker and darker, and wolves had begun to howl nearby, calling him.

"Just leave me alone," he said to himself and turned on to his stomach.

The wounds he had from the foxes were still painful, but he could not care less. They would heal. Teeth burrowed into his skin, close to his spine.

"Howl."

Another set of teeth attacked the right side of his stomach. He was coming under attack from those same foxes again. He jumped up and howled ferociously, in pain. The other wolves ran towards him. Wolfman was bitten many times before Sef's lot ran in, but they saved him in time.

"Catch them. Don't let them go!" Wolfman howled in pain.

The wolves held the two foxes under their paws.

"What shall we do with them?" they asked.

With one paw on his stomach Wolfman frowned. "You must drown them!"

The wolves took the foxes to a nearby river and held their bodies underwater until there was no movement, then let them go. Their bodies were swept away in the fast stream, and that was the end of the wicked foxes.

*

Mr Green learned from the frogs that the foxes had been drowned, a way of dying he had not considered rectifying with his powers.

"Useless foxes! And all of you too! Bring me their bodies!" he shouted.

Once the frogs had located the bodies, a search that took many hours, they offered them to Water Goblin. He kicked them.

"Send them to the girl. That will show her how angry I can get. Wolfman might be next!" He angrily jumped into the pond, upset that he had lost his two mates, vicious mates.

*

Early the next morning, my second day back home, I went out to get some fresh air and to see the sun. I was confronted by the sight of two dead foxes on my doorstep – Water Goblin's best mates. Would he have killed them and sent them to warn me? Was Wolfman all right? What was going on?

My father walked out and saw the dead pair. "They must have wandered off and not been able to find their way back!" he said, but I knew better.

I did not respond to my father's comment but stared at the foxes.

My father placed his arm around my shoulders. "What is it, my child?"

"Nothing, Father, nothing."

I walked back into the house with my father, Dash following close behind.

To be continued...

Anna Paterson - ADL Editorial (Editor)

Lightning Source UK Ltd.
Milton Keynes UK
UKHW011400261021
392872UK00001B/67